At that moment, Judd turned, and Charlie found herself caught in his stare. A long, silent moment passed, and all she could think was,

Lord, don't do this to me again.

Then Judd was laughing between mouthfuls of marshmallows that her daughter was poking into his mouth. Every bite he took, he growled and nipped at her baby fingers, which seemed to the little girl to be the height of hilarity.

When he pulled her toddler out of her car seat and into his arms, Charlie's knuckles went white on the steering wheel. The image of a big strong man carrying her tiny child was too touching to be ignored. At that moment, she would have liked nothing better than to sit there and cry. But letting go of her emotions was a luxury she couldn't afford.

God, please take away this feeling, she prayed silently. *I don't want to want that man....*

Dear Reader,

Once again, Silhouette Intimate Moments brings you an irresistible lineup of books, perfect for curling up with on a winter's day. Start with Sharon Sala's *A Place To Call Home,* featuring a tough city cop who gets away to the Wyoming high country looking for some peace and quiet. Instead he finds a woman in mortal danger and realizes he has to help her—because, without her, his heart will never be whole.

For all you TALL, DARK AND DANGEROUS fans, Suzanne Brockmann is back with *Identity: Unknown.* Navy SEAL Mitchell Shaw has no memory of who—or what—he is when he shows up at the Lazy 8 Ranch. And ranch manager Becca Keyes can't help him answer those questions, though she certainly raises another: How can he have a future without her in it? Judith Duncan is back with *Marriage of Agreement,* a green-card marriage story filled with wonderful characters and all the genuine emotion any romance reader could want. In *His Last Best Hope,* veteran author Susan Sizemore tells a suspenseful tale in which nothing is quite what it seems but everything turns out just the way you want. With her very first book, New Zealander Fiona Brand caught readers' attention. *Heart of Midnight* brings back Gray Lombard and reunites him with the only woman strong enough to be his partner for life. Finally, welcome Yours Truly author Karen Templeton to the line. *Anything for His Children* is an opposites-attract story featuring three irresistible kids who manage to teach both the hero and the heroine something about the nature of love.

Enjoy every one of these terrific novels, and then come back next month for six more of the best and most exciting romances around.

Yours,

Leslie J. Wainger
Executive Senior Editor

Please address questions and book requests to:
Silhouette Reader Service
U.S.: 3010 Walden Ave., P.O. Box 1325, Buffalo, NY 14269
Canadian: P.O. Box 609, Fort Erie, Ont. L2A 5X3

SHARON SALA

A PLACE TO CALL HOME

Silhouette®
INTIMATE™MOMENTS®

Published by Silhouette Books

America's Publisher of Contemporary Romance

SILHOUETTE BOOKS

ISBN 0-373-07973-7

A PLACE TO CALL HOME

Copyright © 1999 by Sharon Sala

This edition published by arrangement with Harlequin Books S.A.

® and TM are trademarks of Harlequin Books S.A., used under license.
Trademarks indicated with ® are registered in the United States Patent
and Trademark Office, the Canadian Trade Marks Office and in other
countries.

Visit us at www.romance.net

Printed in U.S.A.

SHARON SALA

is a child of the country. As a farmer's daughter, her vivid imagination made solitude a thing to cherish. During her adult life, she learned to survive by taking things one day at a time. An inveterate dreamer, she yearned to share the stories her imagination created. For Sharon, her dreams have come true, and she claims one of her greatest joys is when her stories became tools for healing.

I dedicate this book to all of my readers who have vanquished the monsters that slept under their beds.

Chapter 1

"Goddamn it, Hanna, you aren't listening to me."

Detective Judd Hanna of the Tulsa Police Department gave his captain a look that would have quelled a lesser man. Roger Shaw threw up his hands in defeat.

"And don't give me one of those 'spare me' looks, either. This is serious."

Judd let his gaze shift from his captain's face to a spot just over his shoulder, and then the window beyond. There was a window washer halfway up the building across the street. Judd wondered absently why a man would choose such a dangerous occupation.

Shaw saw Judd's focus shift. He turned, following Judd's gaze, saw the man on the scaffolding across the street, and then strode to the windows and deftly dropped the shades. When he turned, Judd was heading for the door.

"I'm not through with you," Shaw snapped. "Get back here now, and that's an order."

Judd sighed. Short of mutiny, which he was considering, disobeying an out-and-out order was beyond him. He turned, wishing that this feeling of helplessness would just go away. He felt aimless…almost out of control. And of all things, Judd Hanna had to be in control. It was the only way he could function.

"What…sir?"

Shaw took a deep breath and then popped a mint in his mouth to keep from cursing again. He'd lost his temper more in the last ten minutes than he had all month. God only knew what his blood pressure was doing right now. He shuddered and pushed the thought from his mind.

"Look, Hanna. I'm serious. This is Vice. We do things here as a team. You can't keep playing cowboy every time we go out on a raid. Use your radio. Call for backup. Depend on your partner. That's why he's there."

Judd's eyes narrowed. "My partner is dead," he said shortly.

Shaw shoved an angry hand through what was left of his thinning hair. Even though Judd had been assigned a new partner over a month ago, he had yet to acknowledge his presence.

"I know it was rough losing Myers the way we did. We all liked Dan. But life goes on. David Sanger is your partner now, and you will, by God, treat him as such."

Judd didn't blink and wouldn't answer. None of them knew the guilt Judd carried. Three days away from retirement, Dan Myers had taken a bullet meant for Judd. Instead of a retirement party, they'd attended Dan's funeral. Judd hadn't slept the night through since.

Shaw glared at the implacable expression on Hanna's face. Never in his life had he wanted to shake anyone as badly as he did right now. And yet looking at him, Shaw knew that was the last thing a sane man would do. At three inches over six feet, and with an attitude that wouldn't quit, Judd Hanna was a man you didn't want to piss off. Shaw sighed, then tried a different approach.

"Hanna, you know as well as I do that the rules are in place for everyone's safety. Not just yours. I don't want to attend another funeral, namely yours."

Judd muttered something that, to Shaw, sounded suspiciously like, who the hell cares.

"That does it!" Shaw snapped. "Turn in your badge and your service revolver. I'm placing you on medical leave until you get your head screwed on straight."

Finally, Shaw had Judd's attention. "You can't!" Judd argued. "We're too close to finding Dan's killer."

Shaw pointed a finger in Judd's face. "That's what I mean," he shouted. "Dan Myers's case belongs to Homicide. We're Vice."

Judd swallowed as panic started to intercede. He couldn't let go just like that. Why couldn't Shaw understand?

"Look, Captain, Dan was my partner. He took a bullet meant for—"

Shaw shook his head. "You heard me. As of this minute, you're on leave…with pay, of course. You will report to Dr. Wilson at nine o'clock tomorrow

morning, and every morning thereafter until he pro-
nounces you fit for duty again.''

The department shrink? Judd's nostrils flared.

"Like hell."

Shaw leaned across his desk, glaring into Hanna's
face.

"Hell it may be," he snapped. "But you don't
come back until Wilson says it's okay."

Judd straightened. Just the notion of letting go of
the devils he lived with was impossible to consider.
He tossed his shield on the desk, then laid his revolver
down beside it. Without saying a word, he headed for
the door.

"Hanna—"

He stopped but didn't turn around, leaving Shaw
to say what must be said to the back of his head.

"Nine o'clock tomorrow morning."

Judd slammed the door behind him. It was all the
comment he was capable of making.

Shaw grabbed the phone and punched in a series
of numbers, frowning as he waited for an answer.

"Dr. Wilson…it's me, Shaw. I've just put Judd
Hanna on medical leave. He's due in your office at
nine in the morning. Yes, he's borderline now. I don't
know what's wrong, but I want it stopped before I
lose him, too."

He hung up, then leaned back in his chair and
closed his eyes. It hadn't been easy being tough on
Hanna. He liked the man, even admired him. And
losing a partner of fifteen years would have been difficult for anyone. At least now things were on the
right track.

But for Judd, everything was off balance. For the
first time since he took the oath of office, he had

nowhere to go but his apartment. He hesitated on the street outside the station house, then headed for the bar down the street. His apartment wasn't home. It was just where he slept, and it was far too early to go to bed.

The bar was cool and fairly quiet. The afternoon crowd had yet to arrive. Judd slid onto a stool and combed his fingers through his hair in frustration. How in hell had his life gotten so mixed up?

"What'll it be?" the bartender asked.

"Bourbon," Judd muttered.

The bartender slid a bowl of pretzels his way and then went to pour the drink. Judd pushed the bowl aside. He didn't need to eat. He needed to forget.

"Here you go, buddy," the bartender said.

Judd grabbed the shot glass and lifted it to his lips, and as he did, he caught a glimpse of his own reflection in the mirror over the bar. But something happened between recognition and focus. Instead of seeing the man that he was, he saw the boy that he'd been. His belly knotted and his heart suddenly ached as he let himself remember.

The pink slip in Joe Hanna's back pocket rode his conscience like a hot poker. Overwhelmed at being fired from another dead-end job, he'd spent the last four hours, and what was left of his money, drowning his sorrows at the local bar. The only thing he had left was a constant, burning rage at the disappointments life had dealt him, and the burden of a ten-year old son he had never wanted.

As he started up the walk to his house, it occurred to him that the house was dark. He squinted against

the glare of streetlights and cursed. That damned kid.
If he wasn't home from school, he would tan his hide.

It never occurred to Joe that more than seven hours
had passed since his son, Judd, would have come
home from school, or that he'd come home to a house
with no food. Joe felt no guilt for his lack of concern.
He kept a roof over their heads, which was more than
his daddy had done for him.

He stumbled as he started up the steps, falling forward and then catching himself on his hands and
knees just before his face hit the porch. A sharp pain
pierced the palm of his right hand. He got up swear-
ing and staggered into the house, turning on the lights,
room by room.

"Boy! Where the hell are you?"

No one answered. Joe cursed again as he stumbled
to the kitchen sink. He looked down at his hand. It
was bleeding. He wiped it on the front of his shirt,
then reached for the cabinet. The second shelf down
from the top was where he kept his liquor. He needed
a drink, but there was nothing there.

He slammed the door shut with a bang. "Goddamn
it, Judd Hanna! You answer me, boy! What did you
do with my whiskey?"

Again, the rooms echoed from the sound of Joe's
voice. Rage grew. His belly burned and his head was
swimming. In a minute, he was going to lie down,
but not before he got his hands on that damned kid.

Joe started through the rooms, shouting Judd's
name. Doors slammed. A lamp tumbled to the floor
and shattered into pieces, and still no sign of the boy.
He was furious. The shame of being fired, coupled
with the frustrations of his life in general, had boiled
into a rage. He staggered back into the kitchen, sway-

ing where he stood and staring around the house in disbelief.

It took a while for him to realize that the door leading down to the basement was slightly ajar. A cold smile broke the anger on his face. Seconds later, he stood at the landing, shouting Judd's name into the darkness below.

The basement walls were damp with condensation, the odors a choking blend of dust and mold. Something scurried in the darkness beneath ten-year-old Judd Hanna's feet and he stifled a gasp. Yet the fear of the unknown was far less sinister to him than the man standing at the landing of the stairs.

"Judd... Judd, boy, I know you're down there. Answer me, damn it."

Judd held his breath, afraid to swallow for fear he'd be heard.

When his father started down the steps, every muscle in Judd's body went tense.

No, no, no... God, don't let him find me.

"Answer me, you sorry little bastard. I know you're down there," Joe growled.

Judd squeezed his eyes shut and shrank a little farther against the wall. If he couldn't see his father, then his father couldn't see him. It was a game he'd played in his mind for more years than he cared to count. Sometimes it worked. Sometimes it didn't.

"What did you do with my whiskey, boy? Answer me, you hear? Don't make me come down there and get you."

Judd gritted his teeth, struggling against the need to cry. It had been years since he'd given his father the satisfaction of knowing he could be hurt.

Joe cursed beneath his breath and reached for the light switch. But nothing happened. He cursed even louder, unaware that Judd had taken the bulb out in hopes he wouldn't be found. But to Judd's dismay, his father started down the steps, fumbling his way through the dark and cursing with every breath.

Judd slid silently to the floor and doubled over on himself, trying to become invisible. His eyes were closed, his breathing almost nonexistent.

"I know you're here," Joe whispered.

Judd's heart was pounding and the bitter taste of fear was in his mouth.

Please God, if you're out there...take me away. Take me away.

"You can't hide from me. Come out now and take your punishment like a man."

Bile rose in the back of Judd's throat. *Please, God, please. Not again. Not again. Don't let him—*

"Gotcha!" Joe said.

When the hand closed around the back of Judd's neck, he knew it was over. He did not go willingly. Fighting against the pain of his father's grasp, he struggled to pull free. If he could get to the stairs, he could get away. He would be safe after that. His father was bound to pass out soon. He always passed out. Those were the only times Judd ever knew peace.

Joe backhanded his son, wincing when one of Judd's teeth accidentally cut the back of his knuckle.

"Don't you bite me, you little bastard," Joe snarled.

Judd's mouth was already swelling as he tried to break free of his father's grasp.

"I didn't mean to, Daddy, I swear."

"Don't lie to me," Joe snapped, and backhanded

him again. "Why didn't you answer me when I called you? And what the hell did you do with my whiskey?"

Reeling from the force of the blows, Judd couldn't think, let alone answer. All he could do was duck and hold up his hands, trying to dodge his father's fists.

It was futile.

Joe was too far gone in his rage to think about what he was doing. In his mind, he was striking out at the man who had fired him and the bartender who'd refused him a last drink. He saw the woman who had laughed at him as he stumbled out of the bar, and himself in a cycle of self-destruction with no way out.

He hated what he saw.

It was the painful jolt of flesh against flesh that finally sank through his senses. Slowly, he became aware that the skin on his hand was stinging. He paused, his arm raised above his head, and looked at the boy who was his son. The child's face was covered in blood. Joe shuddered, his stomach suddenly roiling as the adrenaline rush started to crash. He needed to lie down.

"Now, then," he muttered as he staggered back against the wall. "Let that be a lesson to you."

He expected Judd to run. When he didn't move, Joe shrugged, then turned, grabbing at the stair rail to steady himself. From the faint light spilling out from the stairwell above, he could see that Judd hadn't moved. In fact, the boy's silent demeanor was starting to get to him.

"It's your own fault," he mumbled.

Judd's only response was a slow, careful breath. He would die before he let Joe Hanna know that he hurt.

Joe watched a thick drop of blood gathering at the corner of Judd's nose. He began to get nervous. Tomorrow was a school day. If Judd went to school in this condition, someone might decide to butt into their business. And at this point in Joe's life, he had too much to lose to let that happen.

Joe's wife was dead, worn out by the years of living with the man who had been her husband. And while her death had left him with the burden of raising their son all alone, there had been a benefit to the loss that Joe hadn't expected. Until Judd reached the age of eighteen, he received a monthly social security check on his mother's behalf. And, as Judd's legal guardian, the check came to Joe. It kept a roof over their heads and beer in his belly.

Yet even in the state he was in, Joe had sense enough to realize that if he lost custody of his son, he would lose access to the money. He couldn't let that happen. So, instead of apologizing to his son, he angrily pointed a finger in Judd's face.

"Don't think you're gonna go running to those damned teachers you're so fond of and tattle on me," Joe snarled. "They won't help you. You know why? 'Cause you're white trash, boy, and people don't give a damn about white trash."

Judd's hands curled into fists. A red haze was spreading between himself and his father, and he couldn't think past the heat in his belly. The urge to hit was overwhelming. The urge to wipe that look off his father's face forever was even stronger.

Joe snorted. The kid was a loser. He wouldn't even speak up for himself.

"I'm tired. I'm going to bed now."

Then he started up the stairs. Halfway up, Judd's voice came out of the silence.

"Daddy."

Joe turned, blinking owlishly into the darkness below. Judd was only a vague outline in the shadows.

"What?"

"When you go to bed…say your prayers."

Joe frowned. "What the hell did you say that for?"

"When you sleep, I will kill you."

Joe's lips slackened. The statement was so ludicrous he couldn't think of what to say. But when Judd stepped into the light spilling down from the kitchen above, Joe took an instinctive step back. The hate on his son's face was too real.

He tried to laugh. Judd was just a kid. A ten-year-old kid. But the laughter wouldn't come. Suddenly, he found himself stumbling up the steps and into the light of the kitchen, his heart pounding, his belly lurching. He swayed where he stood, aware that he was only moments from passing out.

When you sleep, I will kill you.

The words still echoed in his head. Suddenly the sound of footsteps coming up the stairs sent him into a panic. Within seconds, he was staggering down the porch steps and running through the bushes of their backyard.

A cat scrambled out of a garbage can, hissing and spitting as Joe stumbled into the alley. The commotion set the neighbor's dog to barking. Joe's blood ran cold. If Judd wanted to, he could find him by the noise trail alone.

Joe paused and looked back. Something moved in the shadows. His heart skipped a beat. He turned and ran and never looked back, passing out some time later beneath some trees in the city park.

When he woke the next morning, his only concern was that he'd outrun his fate. Days after, when the Kentucky authorities came and took Judd away, Joe couldn't bring himself to feel anything but relief.

And Judd Hanna didn't care that his father was out of his life. In his mind, he'd been alone for years. His last refuge had been God, and that night under the stairs, even God had deserted him.

A loud sound outside the bar startled Judd's reverie. He blinked several times as his thoughts refocused. Once more, he found himself staring at the man in the mirror, and at the glass of whiskey only inches away from his lips. He shuddered. Damn. He wasn't far from the man he'd learned to hate.

At that moment, something inside of him snapped. He set the drink down without tasting it, tossed some money on the bar, and headed for the street. His captain had been right. He *was* taking chances with his life, only he didn't know why, but one fact remained that he couldn't ignore. If he wanted to live, it had to stop now.

He walked the streets for hours, weighing his options. His rent was paid until the first of the year and his utility bills were deducted directly from his bank account. He had no one to answer to but himself, and no intentions of spilling his guts to a shrink. In Judd Hanna's mind, that left him only one option, and he was going to take it before it was too late.

Captain Roger Shaw's satisfaction in dealing with Hanna's problem was short-lived. At nine-thirty the next morning, a call from the department shrink verified the fact that Judd Hanna was a no-show.

Furious, he called Judd's apartment and got a disconnect message on the phone. He stared at the receiver in disbelief, then dialed again, certain that he'd made a mistake. Again, the prerecorded message came on, saying that the number he had dialed was no longer in service. By six o'clock that evening, it was obvious that Judd Hanna was gone.

Late August, Call City, Wyoming

Judd Hanna glanced at the map on the seat beside him and then shrugged his shoulders, trying to alleviate some of the tension in his neck. It was the driving. Driving always made him tense. He looked at his watch. It was almost five o'clock. Even though it was a few hours away from nightfall, an early night sounded good. Maybe tonight he would be able to sleep. Maybe tonight the dreams wouldn't come. God, he hoped so. He was tired. So tired.

As he topped a steep hill, he saw movement in the pasture beyond and slowed down to look. It only took a moment for the unfolding scene to register. A little girl of no more than two years old was toddling through the grass. Beyond her, and more than one hundred yards away, was a young woman, running at full stride, with her mouth open in a scream he couldn't hear. To their right, and converging between them and gaining speed with every lope, was a huge black bull. It was obvious to Judd that the baby was the intended target, and that the mother would never reach her in time.

Without thinking, he stomped the accelerator to the

floor. Tires spun on pavement, leaving behind the scent of burning rubber. He bounced across the shallow ditch and then straight through the five-strand barbed wire fence, leaving a tangle of mangled wire and broken fence posts behind him as he went. His grip tightened on the steering wheel as he focused on the dwindling space between the baby and the bull.

Today was laundry day. Two-year old Rachel Franklin loved the days that her mother, Charlotte, pulled all the clothes from the clothes hamper to separate for wash. Charlotte—Charlie to her family— loved her baby more than life, but there were days, like today, when she could have done without her help. She'd already separated the colored clothes twice, each time pulling her red T-shirt from the whites. Rachel did love that red T-shirt, but Charlie didn't think her brother, Wade, would be too fond of pink underwear, especially since he was Call City's chief of police.

"Rachel, give Mommy the shirt," Charlie said.

Rachel picked the red T-shirt from the pile and gave it to Charlie. The smile on her face was so precious that Charlie dropped the clothes she was carrying and picked her daughter up instead, nuzzling her nose against the baby-soft skin beneath Rachel's ear.

Rachel cackled and squealed with delight, then threw her arms around Charlie's neck.

"My mommy," Rachel said, and squeezed as tight as she could.

Charlie returned the hug. "My Rachel," she said, her throat tight with emotion.

The child was her life. The only good thing to

come from loving Pete Tucker, their neighbor's son. He'd played loose with Charlie's feelings, then skipped out on her when she was two months pregnant to chase his dreams on the rodeo circuit. A month before Rachel was born, he'd crawled on a bull that, in a matter of seconds, had put an end to Pete Tucker's dreams.

Charlie had grieved, but only for the loss of Rachel's father. Charlie's love for Pete Tucker had died the day he left her to bear the burden of their affair all alone.

"Want down," Rachel muttered.

Charlie sighed as she put her baby back on her feet. Her daughter's independence was inevitable, but she couldn't help the spear of regret. She tousled Rachel's curls.

"You go play in your room, baby girl. Mommy is going to put these clothes in the washer. Get them all clean for Uncle Wade."

"Unca Wade?"

"Yes, these are for Uncle Wade."

Rachel toddled off, satisfied with her mother's explanation. Next to her mother, Wade Franklin was her favorite person.

Charlie picked up the pile of clothes, careful not to include the red shirt, and headed for the utility room off the kitchen. A couple of minutes later it dawned on her that the house was entirely too quiet and she started back through the rooms in search of Rachel.

"Rachel, where are you?" Charlie called.

She got no answer.

"Rachel, answer Mommy, where are you?"

This time the silence hit hard. Trying not to panic, she retraced her steps, searching in all of Rachel's nooks and crannies, certain she would find her in one of her favorite places.

It wasn't until she'd made the second trip through the house that she noticed the screen door in the living room was slightly ajar. She dashed out on the porch, telling herself to stay calm.

"Rachel, where are you?"

The silence that came afterward was unnerving. She wasted another precious minute running around the house and calling Rachel's name, certain she'd find her playing in the sandbox under the trees in the backyard. But she wasn't there, either.

Now she was beginning to panic. It wasn't until she turned around that she noticed Everett Tucker's black bull was in their pasture again. This wasn't the first time it had happened, and her brother, Wade, had warned Everett more than once to fix his fence. She stood for a moment, staring at the bull's curious stance. His head was up, his body almost motionless in the way animals are when they sense something trespassing on their territory. And then it hit her.

"Oh, God…oh, no," Charlie moaned, and started to run, just as the bull began to charge.

She ran without focus, searching the pasture with a frantic gaze, all the while praying against hope that she was wrong. Then she saw Rachel, toddling through the grass with a handful of flowers. She bolted across the cattle guard, running as she'd never run before, and screaming aloud Rachel's name.

She didn't feel the heat of the sun upon her face. She didn't even hear the sound of her own screams. All she could do was focus on Rachel's curly head and remember how soft her baby's curls were against her face, and how sweet they smelled after a shampoo.

The bull's angry bellow shattered the air and Charlie screamed again, trying to divert his attention. It didn't happen, and it occurred to her then that she would watch her daughter die. As fast as she was running, the bull was still gaining on Rachel, and there was nothing she could do to stop it.

Then out of nowhere, a black Jeep suddenly appeared in the pasture, flying across the ground at breakneck speed. Before she could absorb the implications, she stumbled and fell. The next thing she knew, she was flat on her face. Dirt was in her eyes, and her leg was afire with an unbearable pain. And yet as quickly as she fell, she was struggling to her feet and rubbing at her eyes, desperate to see. Had Rachel died while she was facedown in the dirt?

Through a blur of tears, she looked up to see the Jeep come to a sudden halt only a foot or so from where Rachel was standing. The door opened. She saw a man lean out and yank Rachel inside only seconds before bull and Jeep collided. The heavy thud of bending metal was like music to her ears. She dropped her head and took deep, calming breaths. Nothing mattered any longer. Rachel was safe.

Judd was numb. The rush of adrenaline that had gotten him this far was receding as swiftly as it had come, leaving him weak and shaken. The baby in his arms looked as startled as he'd been moments earlier when he'd seen the scene unfolding. The bull had already done a job on the passenger side of his Jeep and was now butting against the radiator as hard as he could. Judd sighed, watching the steam spewing up from under the hood. No telling what was busted, but it really didn't matter. For now, the child was safe.

He began running his hands over the little girl's body, desperate to assure himself that she had come to no harm. He'd yanked her pretty hard when he'd picked her up, but there hadn't been time for gentle introductions. When he was satisfied that she was all right, he glanced at the bull, who had taken an angry stance a distance away.

So far, so good, Judd thought, and looked around for the woman he'd seen running earlier. Then he saw her on her knees a distance away. It was obvious from the expression on her face that she was in pain.

Beyond the Jeep, the bull began pawing the earth, sending showers of dust into the air. Every now and then, the air would shift from the force of an angry bellow.

Judd eyed the woman nervously. If the bull figured out she was there, she could very well be its next target. Saying a prayer that the Jeep would still move, he grabbed the little girl to keep her from falling, then put it in gear.

"Okay, baby, let's go get your mother."

The little girl stared at Judd with a solemn expression.

"Mommy," she said, pointing with the flowers she still held.

"I see her, honey. And I have a suspicion she would like to see you, too."

The Jeep moved forward amid a spewing mist of steam. He drove slowly, hoping the bull would stay his ground.

Charlie saw them coming, and her heart skipped a beat. The bull stilled, watching intently as the Jeep began to move. She started to get up, and then realized that motion—any motion—might set the bull off. She held her breath, almost afraid to blink. The fire in her ankle was spreading up her leg. When the Jeep stopped beside her, she tried to stand up, then dropped back to the ground from the pain.

A deep, gravelly voice suddenly rumbled close to her ear. "Easy there, lady, let me help."

Charlie was starting to shake. "My baby—"

"She's fine," Judd said. "Put your arms around my neck."

Charlie reacted instinctively, clutching at the collar of his shirt as he picked her up. She had a vague impression of a hard body, dark hair, and a muscle jerking at the side of his jaw as he set her into the driver's side of the seat. Charlie winced as she slid over to the passenger side, grabbing at Rachel as she moved.

"Mommy," Rachel said, and crawled into Charlie's lap as if this was an everyday occurrence.

Charlie clung to her baby in desperation and buried her face in her neck. Seconds later, the door slammed and she knew that the man had climbed back inside. She needed to thank him. She needed to look in his eyes and see the man who had given her back her world, but she couldn't seem to focus on anything but the child in her arms.

Finally, she looked up. Rachel was smiling that sweet baby smile, unaware how close she'd come to getting them both killed.

Charlie stared at a smear of pollen on Rachel's cheek, as well as a crushed petal stuck to the corner of her lip, and didn't know whether to laugh or cry.

Rachel hadn't just been picking the flowers; it looked as if she'd been eating them as well.

Tears welled, spilling down Charlie's face as she wrapped her arms around Rachel, flowers and all, and rocked her where she sat.

"Mommy cwy?" Rachel asked, feeling the streaks on Charlie's cheeks.

Charlie choked on a sob and buried her face in Rachel's curls. "Yes, baby, Mommy's crying. You scared me."

"Fwowers, Mommy. Picked you fwowers."

Charlie nodded and tried to smile, but it was impossible.

Judd saw her distress. The woman was in pain, both emotionally and physically. He looked toward the cluster of buildings just beyond the fence and put the Jeep in gear.

"Hang on, lady. I'm taking you home."

Chapter 2

The farmhouse looked old, but well-cared-for. The single-story white building was a perfect square, with a deep wraparound porch framing the exterior walls. A brown brick chimney rose above the rooftop on the north side of the house. Judd suspected that on a cold winter day the smoke from that chimney would rise high above the grove of surrounding trees.

The woman beside him was still crying, although silently now. He couldn't blame her. For a while there he'd felt like crying himself. As he crossed the cattle guard, the Jeep began to sputter. By the time he got to the house, it was barely moving, but it didn't matter now. They were safe. He killed the engine, then glanced at the woman to his right. There was dirt on her face and blood on her knees, and her fingers were trembling as she brushed at the baby curls tumbling around the little girl's face. In his line of work, he'd seen plenty of people in shock, and he wanted to get her inside before she started coming undone.

"Ma'am, if you'll allow me, I'll help get you inside, and then I'll be needing to use your phone to call for a tow."

Then, what the man had sacrificed to save them hit Charlie. She glanced up, and for the first time, she really looked at him. His eyes were blue—so blue they were almost transparent. His features were even, his jaw strong. There was just a hint of a crook to his nose, an indication of it once having been broken, and there was a small jagged scar on the right side of his jaw. And he was big, so very big. His shoulders spanned almost half the width of the seat. She remembered the feel of his hands closing around her waist and pulling her up to safety, and she shuddered.

"Please, call me Charlie."

He smiled. "I knew a Charlie once, but he wasn't as pretty as you."

It was just the sort of silly remark Charlie needed to gather herself together. "It's short for Charlotte... Charlotte Franklin."

Judd extended his hand. "Pleased to meet you, 'short for Charlotte.' My name is Judd Hanna."

Charlie hesitated, but only briefly. His grasp was firm but gentle, and again, the ordinary gesture took another bite out of her unsettled nerves. She sighed, then pointed to the hood of his car and the smoke spewing out from beneath the hood.

"Mr. Hanna, I'm so sorry about what happened to your car."

"Judd, please," he said, and then looked at Rachel. "As for the damage, it was worth it. Now, let's see about getting you two inside."

He took Rachel out of Charlie's arms and then carried her to the porch.

"Wait right here, honey. We've got to help Mommy, okay?"

"Help Mommy," Rachel echoed, and then sat down on the steps, the wilting flowers still clutched in her hand.

Charlie scooted across the seat and then out from under the steering wheel, but when she tried to stand, her ankle gave way. Before she could argue, Judd picked her up and started up the steps. A little nervous that a total stranger had taken charge of her life, she began to fidget.

"Mr. Hanna, I—"

"Judd."

She sighed. "Judd, this is embarrassing."

He paused. "Lady, allow me the honor of helping one of the bravest people I ever saw."

She flushed. "I don't know what you—"

His voice grew quiet, and the look in his eyes hushed her words.

"You would have both died. You know that, don't you?"

She glanced down at her daughter, who was pulling the petals from a flower, and her expression crumpled.

"Life wouldn't have been worth living without her."

Breath caught in the back of Judd's throat. Logically, he accepted the fact that there were people who would willingly die for another, but Charlotte Franklin's willingness to put herself in harm's way for her child was the first example of that selfless dedication he'd ever seen. He supposed that his mother might once have loved him like that, but he didn't remember it. He glanced back at Rachel, who was still sitting on the steps.

"Yeah. I can only imagine," he said softly. Then he raised his voice a notch. "Come on, little girl, it's time to go inside."

To Charlie's surprise, Rachel minded the stranger and followed them in. As soon as Judd put her down, Rachel crawled up in Charlie's lap and laid her head on her mother's breast.

"Is she okay?" Judd asked.

Charlie nodded. "Just a little confused, I think. She'll be all right." Then she pointed toward the phone. "There's a phone book in the drawer underneath."

Judd shook his head. "You come first. If you don't mind me prowling a bit, I want to put some ice on your ankle."

"The kitchen is that way," Charlie said. "There are some plastic bags in the drawer beside the sink and there's an ice maker in the top of the fridge."

Judd headed for the kitchen, returning shortly with a bag full of ice wrapped in a towel. Charlie winced when he laid it on her ankle.

"Sorry," Judd said. "Does your husband work nearby?"

The tone of Charlie's voice never wavered. "I don't have a husband."

Judd glanced at Rachel, then at Charlie, then fussed with the bag of ice just for something to do.

"I'm sorry, I didn't mean to bring up painful memories. It's just that you can't be here by yourself. Is there anyone I can call for you?"

Charlie sighed. The man was getting the wrong impression, and while it really didn't matter what he thought, she felt obligated to explain.

"I am not a widow. To the contrary, I have never been married. And yes, there is someone—my brother, Wade. If you don't mind handing me the phone, I'll give him a call."

Judd turned, then stopped and stared. "There's a police car coming down your driveway."

A wave of emotion suddenly washed over Charlie. Wade was hardly ever home on time. Thank God this was one of those rare days. To her surprise, she felt tears threatening again.

She took a deep breath, trying to still the tremble in her voice. "That would be Wade. He's the police chief in Call City."

Judd stiffened, then made himself relax, accepting the irony of the situation. He'd driven halfway across the country to get away from law enforcement, and the first time he lingered long enough to exchange names, they were tied to the same damned branch of government.

A few moments later, the officer who'd been driving the car came through the door, his eyes wide with concern. Judd braced himself for the confrontation.

Wade had been looking forward to an easy evening until he'd seen the destruction to the pasture fence. His mood had taken a quick swing downward and was far from level when he came through the door. Seeing Charlie's tears and the stranger standing next to her, his hand automatically slid to the butt of his gun.

"Charlie…honey…what the hell happened?"

"It's okay," Charlie said, and then started to cry in earnest.

Judd sighed. She'd been bordering on hysteria ever since he'd pulled her out of the dirt. It was inevitable that she would finally break down. What surprised him was the urge he had to comfort her.

Wade moved toward Charlie, but his attention was completely focused on the man standing next to her.

"Easy, buddy," Judd said, "I'm the good guy here." Then he offered his hand. "My name is Judd Hanna."

Wade nodded, but reserved the right to the handshake until after he knew some more facts. Judd shrugged. He couldn't really blame him.

"What the hell happened to the fence?" Wade said, looking straight at Judd. "Did it run into your car?"

Judd laughed out loud. Even Charlie managed to chuckle through tears. Rachel giggled, too, although the joke was over her head, and then she pointed out the door.

"Big bull."

Wade frowned. "What bull, honey?"

Charlie choked on a sob. "Oh, Wade. Tucker's bull…it was in our pasture again. I couldn't find Rachel, and then I saw her…and the bull was charging…but I couldn't outrun…if it hadn't been for…he drove through the fence and…I fell and it was…oh, God, Wade, the bull would have killed her."

She shuddered, then buried her face against the back of Rachel's neck.

All the color faded from Wade Franklin's face. He looked at Judd, and this time, he was the one who offered his hand.

"Mister, I suppose we'll sort out the details later, but if I'm understanding the situation here, you just saved their lives, and if that's so, then there aren't enough words to thank you."

Judd shrugged, a little embarrassed at being the sudden focus of attention. "I just happened to be in the right place at the right time."

Too overcome to speak, Wade impulsively hugged him. Judd was still reeling from the impact of being royally thumped on the back when Wade let him go and shifted his focus to Charlie.

He squatted down beside her and lifted the ice from her foot. "I think you need to see a doctor," he said, then took out his handkerchief and wiped at the tears and dirt on her face as if she was a child.

Charlie caught his hand. "No, it's just a sprain. I'll be fine."

Judd's heart twisted again. The closeness between brother and sister only served as a reminder of what was missing in his life.

"About that phone call," Judd said. "If you'd recommend a towing service and a motel, I'll be out of your hair."

Wade rocked back on his heels. "There aren't any motels in Call City, and the only tow truck is out on a call. I know because I sent him."

Then he glanced at Charlie. She nodded. They had no options but to offer their home to the man. After all he'd done, it was the least they could do.

"Charlie and I would consider it an honor to put you up for the night."

Judd shook his head. "That's not necessary. I've slept in my car plenty of times. It won't hurt me to do it again."

"No," Charlie said. "You'll stay in the house, with us."

He took a deep breath and looked down. Even with the dirt on her face, Charlotte Franklin was a good-looking woman, but it was the expression in her eyes that swayed him. She needed to make reparation. Whether he wanted to or not, he felt obligated to accept her hospitality.

"Then I thank you," he said. "And just to make sure you folks don't feel the need to sleep with a gun under your pillow, would it make you feel better to know I'm a cop?"

Wade's smile was one of relief as he stood abruptly. "Why didn't you say so sooner?"

"Probably because I'm AWOL from my precinct," Judd said. "And, before you assume the worst, I'm not in trouble, I just got fed up."

Wade's gaze narrowed thoughtfully. "Yeah, that can happen."

Judd handed Wade a card with the phone number on it.

"Call the Tulsa, Oklahoma, P.D. Ask for Captain Roger Shaw. He'll vouch for my honesty, if not my sanity."

Charlie flinched, then held her baby closer, suddenly unsure of having this stranger in their house all night. Judd caught the look.

"Ma'am."

She looked up.

"I swear to you that the only person I'm capable of hurting is myself."

Charlie stared intently. She had no reason to trust his word, other than the fact that he'd saved their lives. It would have to be enough. Finally, she nodded and managed a smile.

"Then that's that," Wade said. "And before you call a mechanic, I need to use the phone. I've got to talk to a man about a bull."

Wade stalked to the phone and punched in some numbers before taking the portable with him as he strode out to the porch.

Charlie combed a shaky hand through her hair as Rachel wiggled to be put down. Through the open doorway, bits and pieces of Wade Franklin's conversation could be heard.

"Don't give a good damn about why...nearly killed...going to be hamburger if you don't get the son of a..."

Charlie looked at Judd and then sighed. "Wade has a bad temper."

Judd shrugged. "I don't blame him. If it had been me, I would have probably shot the son of a bitch and worried about the complications later."

Startled by his matter-of-fact tone, Charlie could think of nothing to say. When Judd turned away, she found herself watching his every move.

"Potty," Rachel suddenly announced.

Charlie groaned. With her bad ankle, she'd never make it to the bathroom with Rachel in time.

"Wade! Come quick."

Her call brought her brother running.

"What's wrong?" he asked.

"Rachel needs to go to the bathroom."

Wade laughed and tossed the cell phone on the cushion beside Charlie as he picked up his little niece.

"Come on, shortcake, let's hurry."

Rachel giggled. "Hurry, hurry," she repeated.

Charlie rolled her eyes and then glanced at Judd. He was grinning.

"Potty training," she explained. "There's never much time between her and disaster."

His grin widened.

"As soon as Wade comes back, he'll show you where you can sleep. After I wash some of this dirt off myself, I'll see to fixing supper."

"No, ma'am," Judd said. "We'll cook. You just sit there and look pretty. It'll make us all feel better."

Charlie blushed. Moments later, Wade was back. He helped her to her feet and then down the hall to the bathroom, leaving Rachel and Judd alone.

Judd squatted until he was eye to eye with the little girl, and then reached out and pulled a flower petal from the side of her face.

"These any good?" he asked, and licked it.

She giggled and ducked her head.

As she smiled, the knot in Judd's belly shifted slightly. Maybe this detour wouldn't be so bad, after all.

Within the hour, Judd realized how unimportant haste was in Call City. It would be morning before the mechanic would come get his car. Even if he'd been willing to pay the extra money to have it hauled in tonight, it would solve nothing. The garage wouldn't be open until 7:00 a.m., so there was no need to hurry just to have it parked.

Resigned to his fate, he'd taken his suitcase out of the Jeep and headed for the room he'd been given. It was small but clean, and the furniture was sturdy. The fact that he'd have to share a bathroom with a baby and two other people seemed a small price to pay for the comfort of a home-cooked meal and a place to wash some clothes.

A short while later, Judd saw a pickup truck coming down the driveway and pulling a trailer. The owner of the runaway bull, he assumed. He watched from the window as Wade met the man in the drive. Again, harsh words were traded, and while he was debating with himself about getting involved before someone threw the first punch, he overheard something that stunned him. The man called Tucker wasn't only the owner of the bull, he was Rachel Franklin's grandfather, as well. What made no sense was that he was so belligerent about the fact.

"He's not a happy man," Charlie said, pointing toward the man in the truck.

Startled, Judd turned. "Who, Wade?"

"No, Everett Tucker."

Judd turned away, a little embarrassed at being caught eavesdropping, but he supposed it was the cop in him, always wanting to know the why of everything.

"I didn't intend to pry," he said.

Charlie shrugged. "It's no secret in these parts that Everett doesn't like us." Then she turned and looked at Rachel, who was playing on the floor in front of the television. "He especially doesn't like Rachel."

"But why?" Judd asked.

"Because she's all there is left of his only son, Pete, and I guess it hurts him too much to look at her."

"I'm sorry," Judd said. "Again, I seem to be stepping on ghosts."

Charlie glanced at him and managed a smile. "No. All my ghosts are laid, Mr. Hanna. It wasn't in me to grieve for Pete's death when he'd already walked out on me for getting pregnant.''

Judd paled. ''Look, I know I keep saying this, but I'm sorry. And for what it's worth, the man must have been a purebred fool.''

Charlie sighed. ''Pretty much.''

Uncomfortable with the emotions tumbling around in his head, Judd stared at her for a moment, then strode out the door.

The sun was hanging low in the west before Judd came back in the house. He'd helped Wade mend the fence, but did little more than watch as the livestock were fed. Country life was something foreign to his world.

After washing up, Wade had handed him a bowl of potatoes and a paring knife and then headed for the door with a platter of steaks. Now he stood at the sink peeling potatoes while Wade tended to the meat cooking on the grill outside. Judd watched as Rachel ran from the swing set to her uncle and back again, talking nonstop without care if anyone answered. He paused with a potato in one hand and the paring knife in the other, imagining himself in such a family tableau. Then reality surfaced and he returned to the potatoes, removing the peelings in angry chunks. It was obvious as hell that he couldn't take care of himself, let alone a wife and kids, so why want something he couldn't have?

In the midst of his anger, it dawned on him he was no longer alone. He pivoted. Charlotte Franklin was standing in the doorway, using the facing for a crutch. He dropped the knife and potato and bolted toward her, wiping his hands on his jeans as he went.

"You shouldn't be on that foot. Let me help you to a chair."

Grateful for his strength, Charlie started to lean on him, when Judd slid an arm beneath her shoulders and lifted her off her feet.

"This is getting embarrassing," she muttered.

Judd grinned, trying to put her at ease. "Now, Charlie, you wouldn't deny a man such a golden opportunity. It isn't every day I get the excuse to hold a pretty woman."

"Not even your wife?"

Judd found himself caught in her gaze. For a long moment, neither moved—neither spoke. Damp tendrils of her freshly washed hair brushed the backs of his hands. Her eyes were wide and questioning, her expression tense, as if she were holding her breath for an answer she didn't want to hear. Then he shook off the thought. This was crazy. She was a stranger.

"Not married," he said, and then added, "No significant other, either. Being a cop isn't conducive to permanent relationships."

"You can put me down now," she said.

Judd blinked, a bit startled by the abrupt change in their conversation, and then continued his trek across the floor, gently lowering her into a chair.

"Thank you," she said.

He nodded. As he started back toward the sink, she spoke.

"Mr. Hanna..."

He sighed, then turned. Obviously she wasn't going to call him Judd until she was ready.

"Yes?"

"It isn't the job, it's the man inside the uniform that controls his own life."

Reeling from the brutal truth in her words, he was still struggling for an answer when Wade came inside.

"Steaks are done," he announced, carrying the platter before him as if he were bearing pure gold.

"The potatoes aren't," Judd said, and headed for the sink.

Charlie stared at the stiff set to Judd's shoulders, and ignored her brother's curious gaze. Obviously, her comments had touched a nerve.

"No matter. These will keep," Wade said. "I've got to fish Rachel out of the sandbox, anyway." He set the plate down on the table near Charlie's elbow and headed back out the door.

The evening meal came and went, but long after Judd had gone to bed that night, Charlotte Franklin's words still rang in his ears. *It isn't the job, it's the man inside the uniform that controls his own life.*

If that was true, then no wonder he thought he was going crazy. That night he dreamed of his partner, Dan Myers—laughing one minute, then the next, drowning in his own blood from the bullet that had exploded inside his chest.

Judd was in the country, so awakening to the crow of a rooster didn't surprise him. But he wasn't expecting to feel soft baby breath on the side of his face. One heartbeat he was drifting toward consciousness and the next second he was wide-awake and staring into a pair of round brown eyes. Before he could move, Rachel Franklin stuck her finger up his nose.

"Nose," she said.

He laughed. It wasn't the soft, easy chuckle that his buddies in the department would have recognized. In fact, if he'd heard a replay of it, he wouldn't have recognized himself. It was a deep, from-the-belly laugh that echoed within the silence of the house. The little girl giggled and ducked her head behind the blanket wadded up in one arm, then peeked out at him again.

He reached down and picked her up, sitting her on the side of the bed. Soft baby curls straggled down in her eyes, and she was missing a sock. But she smelled sweet and the smile she gave him was even sweeter.

"So, you're an early bird, are you, punkin?"

"Bird," Rachel said, and pointed out the window.

Judd's grin widened. She wasn't just pretty. She was smart, too. It shouldn't have mattered, but the knowledge pleased him.

"Yeah, that's right. Birds live in trees."

She wiggled her bottom a little closer to the warmth of his leg beneath his covers, and pulled her blanket up under her chin just as Charlie came hobbling into the room.

Her hair wasn't in much better shape than her daughter's, but that was where the similarities ended. Devoid of all makeup and with eyes still heavy with sleep, she had the look of a woman who'd spent the night in a loving man's arms. He had a moment of insanity wondering what it would be like to make love to her, and then tossed it aside.

"I am so sorry," Charlie said as she made a grab for Rachel. "She's just started getting out of her baby bed by herself."

Judd grinned. "If you could bottle her action, she'd make alarm clocks passé."

"I'm afraid to ask, but what did she do?" Charlie asked.

Judd grinned. "Let's just say that, if it wasn't before, I'm pretty sure my left nostril is clean."

Charlie rolled her eyes. "Oh, Lord."

Judd started to laugh again. "It wasn't so bad. It's better than the barrel of a .45, any day."

Charlie grimaced. "You cops have a weird sense of humor. Now, if you'll excuse us, we'll leave you to your sleep."

Judd stretched and yawned. "Never was much good at sleeping in," he said. "If you don't mind, I'll make some coffee."

Charlie's pulse gave a leap as the sheet slipped down toward his belly. It was all she could do to answer.

"Uh...yes...I mean, no, I don't mind. Make yourself at home. Wade is in the shower but he'll be out in a few minutes."

Judd glanced down at her ankle as she moved toward the door. It was still swollen and starting to bruise. Without thinking, he started to get up and help her, then remembered he had nothing on. He waited until they were gone, then got up and dressed, keeping it casual. He put on his last pair of clean jeans and a slightly wrinkled T-shirt bearing the logo of the Tulsa P.D.

As he headed for the kitchen, he could hear Charlotte's voice, soft and coaxing as she helped her daughter dress, as well as the occasional rumble of Wade Franklin's voice. From what he could hear, the police chief was already on the phone, dealing with the business of the day. Just for a moment, he regretted the fact that he wasn't getting ready for the job, then reminded himself that it was because of the damned job that he was here. Somehow, he was going to have to find a way to forgive himself for not dying along with Dan Myers.

A couple of minutes later, he was digging through the cabinets for the coffee when Wade walked into the kitchen. He turned.

"I asked Charlie if it would be okay to make coffee," he said.

Wade shrugged, obviously preoccupied. "Have at it," he muttered.

Judd filled the carafe with water then measured out the coffee, all the while keeping an eye on Wade. Once the coffee was on and brewing, he turned.

"Got trouble?" he asked.

Wade nodded. "Probably."

"Want to talk about it?"

Wade reached for a bottle of painkillers. "Bad knee," he said, and downed a couple without water.

Judd waited. If the man wanted to talk, he would do so when he was ready. Then Wade looked up, and Judd felt himself under sudden scrutiny.

"I talked to your captain," Wade said.

Judd grinned wryly. "What did he say?"

"That he was glad to know the son of a bitch was still alive and to tell him to get his ass back to Tulsa."

Judd shrugged. "He loves me. What can I say?"

Wade almost grinned, but there was more on his mind than Judd's defection.

"He also said you're a hell of a detective, which brings me to my question."

Suddenly, Judd sensed he wasn't going to like what was coming.

"Looks like I've got myself a problem in Call City," Wade said, then poured them each a cup of coffee before continuing. "A man named Raymond

Shuler, who is president of the local bank, is missing. His wife said he went to a meeting last night and never came home. My deputy found his car, still parked at the town hall where the meeting was held, but Shuler is nowhere to be found.''

Judd frowned. ''This ever happened before?''

Wade shook his head. ''That's just it. Shuler isn't the type to pull any stunts. It's obvious something has happened.''

''Like robbery, or maybe another woman?''

Wade shrugged. ''Could be any number of things. I'll find out more when I get to the office.''

''What's that have to do with me?'' Judd asked.

Wade paused. Judd could see the hesitation on his face.

''It's just that my deputy, Hershel Brown, is getting married tomorrow and leaving on his honeymoon. He won't be back for at least two weeks, maybe more. I can hardly ask the kid to postpone his wedding because of this, and I'm damned sure not going to tell him he can't go on his honeymoon, but I'm going to be real shorthanded until he gets back.''

Judd stiffened. ''How many other deputies do you have?''

Wade grinned. ''None, and since you're going to be stuck here until your Jeep is fixed, I thought you might consider helping me out with this case. I could probably work a small consultation fee into the budget, although it wouldn't be much.''

Judd sighed. This wasn't what he'd planned to do, but like the man said, what other options did he have?

Then Wade added the kicker. ''And, since you'll be staying on here until your vehicle is up and running…''

"Okay," Judd said. "But no fee is necessary. Technically, I'm still employed in Oklahoma."

Wade grinned. "Thanks, man, I really appreciate this."

"Don't thank me yet," Judd said.

Wade shrugged off the warning, but before he could comment, someone honked outside.

Wade refilled his coffee cup and then motioned with his chin. "That will be Tooter Beel."

"Tooter?"

Wade grinned. "Don't ask." Then he added, "He'll tow your car to the garage in town, but you'll have to wait until tomorrow to talk to the mechanic."

Judd frowned. This meant another day's delay added on to the rest. Then he sighed. Why wasn't he surprised?

"Why tomorrow?" he asked.

"Because today is Monday and Harold doesn't open the shop on Mondays."

Judd knew he shouldn't ask, but the question came out, anyway.

"And why doesn't he open on Mondays?"

Wade's grin widened. "Because he's usually sleeping off a weekend drunk. Even if he came in and unlocked the shop, you wouldn't want him working on anything. He's real mean until the liquor wears off."

"So, all that's going to happen today is my Jeep gets parked in town?"

"That's about the size of it."

"Fine. Then I'll stay here and help Charlie."

Wade looked nervous. This wasn't what he had in mind.

"Uh, I don't think…"

"Is there anyone…maybe a neighbor, or a friend, who can come stay with her?" Judd asked.

Wade frowned. "No."

"Maybe you were planning to stay here and help her?" Judd asked.

"Not with Shuler missing. In fact, I should already be at the office," Wade said.

"So, what's-his-name can tow my car and I'll stay here and help. Maybe by tomorrow the swelling in her foot will be down."

The horn sounded again. Wade was out of excuses. He set his coffee cup down and headed for the door.

"Fine," he said shortly. "I'll tell Tooter to hook 'er up and pull it into town. You can talk to Harold tomorrow about repairs."

"Sounds like a plan to me," Judd said, and wondered why he'd been so bent on baby-sitting a woman and a kid. It wasn't like him. In fact, it wasn't like him at all.

Chapter 3

Judd couldn't remember ever wanting to touch a woman as much as he wanted to touch Charlotte. Her skin, an even golden tan, was glistening with a faint sheen of perspiration as she crawled around on her knees, weeding the flower garden in front of the house. She wore her hair in a thick rope of braid, and the warm chestnut color glowed from the heat of the sun. The braid hung over her shoulder as she worked, and each time she straightened to rest her back, it would bounce against the thrust of one breast. Her shorts were old and frayed at the hems, the denim fabric faded by countless washings, and the logo on her T-shirt was completely illegible. He kept staring at the slender curve of her neck and the high, delicate instep of her small bare feet, and telling himself to focus on something else. He didn't listen.

Beyond the sandstone walk, the baby played, carrying a small bucket of dirt from one pile to another, then scooping it up and doing it all over again. Overhead, a lone turkey buzzard circled high in the sky, looking for something to eat. Judd glanced up, past the buzzard to the jet trail far above, and thought of the faceless people in that plane. They didn't know it, but at this very moment, they were flying over heaven.

"Judd, would you hand me that small rake, please?"

He grabbed at the rake with a guilty conscience. Could she tell he'd been thinking about her? Would it show on his face?

"Thanks," she said, and began pulling it through the dirt, loosening the soil around the roots of some bushes.

"I would have been happy to do that for you," Judd said.

Charlie paused, giving him more than a casual glance. His shoulders were straining at the shirt he was wearing, and from where she was sitting, the muscles in his legs weren't too shabby, either. She wondered if he was a fitness freak, and then discarded the thought. It shouldn't matter to her what he was.

"Do you know the difference between marigolds and weeds?" she asked.

He hesitated and then grinned. "No."

"Then if you don't mind, I'll do it myself."

Judd laughed. "You don't trust men much, do you?"

She never looked up. "I haven't had much reason."

Judd's smile faded. He glanced at Rachel, watching the way her baby curls bounced as she toddled from place to place, and he thought of the fool who'd denied her.

"No, I guess you haven't at that," he said softly, watching as Rachel came toward them, still carrying her shovel but leaving her little bucket behind.

"Mommy, I sirsty."

"Just a minute, sweetie," Charlie said. "Let Mommy get up and I'll get you a drink."

Judd put his hand on her shoulder. "I would be happy to take her for you."

Charlie hesitated, then smiled. "Thanks, but I'd better do it. She probably needs to go to the bathroom, too."

Judd started to argue, then thought better of it. He couldn't blame her. If it was his daughter, he wouldn't want a strange man taking her to the bathroom, either.

He nodded, then slid his hands beneath her armpits and pulled Charlie to her feet. For a second, they were face-to-face, gazes locked.

Then something happened.

Charlie would think later that it was a recognition of souls, while Judd would not remember the thought in his mind, only the yearning to kiss her.

He moved.

She lifted her face and held her breath.

"Mommy…"

Rachel's plea yanked them back to reality, a vivid reminder that they were not alone. Desperate to put something between them, Judd picked the child up, then slid his free arm around Charlie's waist and helped her into the house. Oddly enough, she leaned on his strength without fuss, taking his help as it was meant to be given. When they were inside, he set Rachel down in the hall outside the bathroom door.

Charlie moved past him without comment. Judd watched the door closing between them while thinking he should have gone into town with Wade, after all. Staying alone in this house with Charlotte Franklin hadn't been a good idea. He already admired her. He didn't want to like her—at least, not so much that it would matter when it was time to leave.

Raymond Shuler came to in the dark and thought at first he'd gone blind. Then he felt the blindfold on his eyes and fought an urge to throw up. A whimper of protest came up his throat, but never got past the gag in his mouth. The ropes around his wrists and ankles were rough and binding, but those were the least of his worries. He'd been kidnapped. He was going to die.

Time passed. His mind was clearing as he recognized a current of air moving across his skin. A few seconds later it hit him. My God, he was naked!

Fear sliced through him, leaving him sick to his stomach as he struggled to pull free. The smell of dust was thick in the air and his throat felt dry, his lips cracked and burning.

Something rattled—then rattled again. At the sound of footsteps, he stilled. Was this it? Was this the moment he was going to die? He thought of his wife, of his family, of the debts that he owed and the secrets he'd kept and wondered how the world could go on without him. A low whimper slid up his throat, hanging just behind the gag stuffed in his mouth.

Hands yanked him roughly, rolling him from his back to his belly. He started to cry, mutely begging for a mercy that never came. Suddenly, something hot was thrust against his hip and the scent of burning flesh was in the air. Shocked by the unexpected stab of piercing pain, he arched up off the floor and then blessedly passed out before it was over. He never knew when the syringe full of antibiotic went into his arm, or when the sound of footsteps receded. It would be another day before he awoke, and by that time, the deed—and the damage—had been done.

"So, what do you know about the missing banker that you didn't know this morning?" Judd asked as he cleared the table from the supper they'd just had.

Oblivious to the seriousness of the conversation going on around her, Rachel crawled up on her uncle Wade's lap and began unbuttoning his shirt—a new and favorite pastime.

Wade looked down at his niece and grinned as her tiny fingers worked the buttons out of the holes.

"Not much," he said. "Only that it looks like a real abduction, but there's been no demand for ransom."

"Does he have money?" Judd asked.

Charlie snorted lightly. "He's got plenty of ours," she muttered.

Wade patted Charlie on the hand, then looked at Judd. "Sometimes it's hard to meet the mortgage payments and Shuler isn't exactly a 'good old boy' when it comes to extensions." Then he answered Judd's question. "Yeah, he's got money. Inherited it from his old man."

Judd frowned. "Maybe you're not the only people who don't like the way he does business. Would you say he has enemies?"

Charlie's snort was a little more pronounced. "It

would be easier to count his friends. There're fewer of them."

Judd grinned at her. Damned if he didn't like her spunk. "That bad, is he?"

She grimaced, then looked at Wade and sighed. "Am I being dramatic again?"

"Yes, honey, but that's part of why I love you."

She grinned. "And the other part is?"

He looked down at the imp in his lap. His chest was bare clear down to his belt. When she started twisting the hair on his chest around her little fingers and pulling, he yelped, then handed her to Charlie.

"I suppose that would be Miss Rachel here, although I must be a masochist for thinking it. Every night I suffer the tortures of the damned with those tiny fingers." He looked at Judd and grinned. "With Rachel, who needs a razor?"

"Or a handkerchief," Judd added.

Charlie thought of the way Judd had been awakened this morning and started to laugh.

"What did I miss?" Wade asked.

"While you were in the shower this morning, Judd had a rather rude awakening."

Wade started to grin. "Not the finger-up-the-nose trick?"

Judd chuckled. "Oh, yeah," he said. "But it was the exploratory twist before she pulled it out that got my full attention."

Wade chuckled as Charlie squeezed Rachel close in her arms, burying her nose against the little girl's neck.

"You're such a mess, baby girl. What is Mama going to do with you?"

Judd leaned over and patted the tousle of curls on

Rachel's head. They felt like loops of silk against his palm.

"Just love her," he said softly. "These days, the age of innocence is far too short."

Wade's smile slipped. "Amen to that," he said, and then out of curiosity, decided to change the subject. "So, you know how my day went. What did you two do?"

"Not much," Charlie said, and began fussing with the ties on Rachel's tennis shoe.

"She did a little gardening," Judd added, and stacked the rest of the plates in the sink.

The stilted tones of their voices set Wade on alert. For a moment he sat, staring at them in disbelief. Charlie was tying Rachel's laces in knots and Judd began splashing water far too forcefully for the small stack of dishes that had to be washed. Concern crept into his thoughts. Despite the fact that the man was a cop and had saved Rachel's life, he was still a stranger. Had he done something to Charlie while he was gone?

The chair squeaked across the linoleum as he suddenly stood.

"That's the biggest bunch of nothing I ever heard and I've heard a lot. What went on out here that no one wants to discuss?"

Charlie stood, meeting her brother's angry gaze. "Oh, for Pete's sake, Wade, do you honestly think that if Judd had been less than a gentleman, he would be standing in my kitchen in one piece? I thought you knew me better than that."

Judd was almost as angry, but at himself for getting into this position.

"Look, you two. Just give me a ride into town and I'll be out of your lives for good."

Panic hit Charlie hard as she turned toward him, and in that moment, she accepted the fact that she didn't want him to go. But before she could speak, Wade shrugged and grinned.

"Sorry I jumped to conclusions. I guess it's my suspicious nature. I've been a cop too long." Then he added. "Besides, you can't go. You promised to help me with the Shuler case."

Judd nodded without comment. The way he figured, the less said, the better. Technically, Charlie was right. Nothing had happened. But they both knew it could have, and that was where the guilt began.

Morning of the next day dawned gray and overcast. Charlie slipped out of bed, gingerly testing her weight on her ankle. It was markedly better, which was, to her, a relief. Having Judd Hanna for a houseguest was difficult enough when Wade was around to play buffer, but being alone with him had been worse. There was something about him that she couldn't let go. At first, she thought it was gratitude for the fact that he'd saved their lives. But that theory hadn't lasted past the first time she'd thought about kissing him. She'd been grateful to a lot of people in her lifetime, but she hadn't once wanted to kiss them the way she'd wanted to kiss Judd Hanna.

All night she'd struggled with her conscience. Sometime around morning, she had decided that she didn't want to be thinking of a man. The last time she'd let her guard down with one, she'd wound up with a baby and no husband. That wasn't happening to her again.

She dressed quietly, hoping to get into the kitchen and start breakfast before Rachel woke up. Considering the weather, she opted for a pair of blue jeans rather than shorts, and tucked her T-shirt into the waistband before giving herself a last look in the mirror. Her hair was neatly braided, her clothes were old but clean. She'd even managed to get an old sandal onto her swollen foot without too much discomfort. But as she exited her bedroom, she kept feeling as if she was leaving something undone. And then Judd walked out of his room and for a startled moment, they were alone in the hallway.

Judd started to speak, when Charlie put a finger to her lips and shushed him before leading him into the kitchen.

"Rachel," she explained, pointing back down the hall. "She's a light sleeper."

He nodded, but his thoughts were on the uneven row of tiny curls already popping out from her neat hairdo and feathering across her forehead.

Charlie reached for the coffeepot and began filling it with water. He was making her nervous.

"Did you sleep well?" she asked.

"Yes."

The silence between them was noticeable.

"How's your foot?" Judd finally asked.

She turned, a fake smile on her face. "Better, thanks."

Now the lull in the conversation was uncomfortable.

Finally, they both turned to speak at once, then laughed uncomfortably.

"You first," Charlie said.

Judd shook his head. "No, ma'am. Ladies first."

She set a skillet on the stove, then took a bowl of eggs from the refrigerator.

"Scrambled okay with you?"

He grinned wryly. "It pretty much fits the description of my brain, so I guess that sounds about right."

Charlie stopped. This wasn't the first time he'd made light of his exodus from his job. She suspected he wasn't really as carefree about it as he claimed.

She set the eggs down. "Can I ask you something?"

He shrugged. "Have at it."

"What happened to you?"

His smile faded. "Hell if I know," he said, and turned away.

"I'm sorry," Charlie said. "It's really none of my business."

Judd sighed and made himself face her again. "My partner died on the eve of his retirement. He took a bullet meant for me and I can't get the memory of his wife's face out of my head."

"Oh, Judd…"

He grimaced. "That's exactly what she said when I told her Dan was dead."

"Being a cop is a dangerous occupation," she said. "He knew the risks. So did his wife."

Judd digested her answer. Logically, he knew she was right, but logic and emotions rarely went hand in hand.

"Charlotte?"

Charlie looked up. Rarely did anyone call her by her full name, but hearing the syllables roll softly out of Judd's mouth gave her shivers.

"Yes?"

"Can I ask *you* something?"

She hesitated, then managed a smile and nodded. "Sure, why not?"

"Did you love Rachel's father?"

Her smile twisted bitterly. "Once, when I was still naive enough to believe people meant what they said."

Judd flinched. He understood her anger, but was surprised by the answering chord he felt within himself. He knew firsthand the pain of abandonment and lies. Impulsively, he touched the side of her face.

"I'm sorry."

Charlie froze, telling herself to ignore the warmth of his palm against her cheek and the tenderness in his voice.

"You have nothing to apologize for," she said shortly, and turned away before she made a fool of herself.

Judd sighed. He felt sad, frustrated, even though he understood her unwillingness to compromise. She'd done it once and look what had happened.

And then the sound of little footsteps pattering down the hall broke the mood. Moments later, Rachel came into the kitchen, her blanket bunched under her arm like a sack and her thumb in her mouth. Her curls were in tangles and, once again, she was missing a sock. She was so endearing, he reached down and picked her up. Without thinking, he nuzzled his nose against the side of her neck, inhaling the sweet baby scent, and gave her a soft kiss on the cheek.

"Good morning, punkin. What's that you have in your mouth?"

Then he teased at her thumb, tugging gently without intending to remove it from her mouth. The unexpected game brought a giggle out of Rachel that warmed Judd's heart.

Charlie was mesmerized by what she was seeing. The trust her daughter had just given to Judd was surprising, as was the lump in Charlie's throat. All she could think was, so this was what their lives would have been like if Pete Tucker had been a different man. Rachel would have had a father and she would have had a—

She inhaled sharply and reached for the eggs, angrily breaking them one by one into a bowl. Stop it, she warned herself. Stop it right now. Fantasizing was one thing, but letting it go too far could be dangerous.

Wade came in on Rachel's heels, and soon the kitchen was full of noise and laughter and Rachel begging for something to eat. And in the midst of it all, Judd sat, quietly watching and absorbing the love that bound them. Wade left soon afterward in his patrol car, leaving Judd to ride into town later with Charlie. The day was already full of things to be done. Charlie had shopping to do. Rachel had a checkup at the doctor's. Wade had a missing man to find, and Judd needed to see a man about fixing his Jeep. Ordinary things on an ordinary day. But why, Judd wondered, if it was so ordinary, did he feel as if he was on the brink of discovery?

Waves of pain rolled across Raymond Shuler's leg and up the muscles in his back. He'd lost track of time. Living behind the blindfold and gag was disorienting. Day turned to night, then back to day again. Every time he began to come to, someone poked a needle in his butt and sent him back to La La Land, which was fine with him. Lack of consciousness made his situation more bearable. He knew little more than he had when he'd first been taken, other than the fact that he was still naked, and whatever they'd done to his hip was probably infected. The heat from the wound permeated his entire body, often racking him with fever and chills. The mattress on which he was lying belly-down smelled like chicken feathers and dust. If he hadn't been so sick, he would have been starving. Except for water, not a morsel of sustenance had passed his lips since this nightmare began. Every now and then when lucidity came, he would try to figure out who could have possibly done this to him.

In his business, he made enemies, but it went with the territory of being a banker. However, as hard as he had tried, he couldn't think of one single man he'd pissed off who had enough guts to carry this through. So where did that leave him? Tied up and hurting in some godforsaken place, that's where. All he could do was pray that, one way or another, it would soon be over.

Judd exited the body shop, satisfied that his vehicle was in good hands. Now all he had to do was exhibit some patience. It would take a week, maybe longer, for the parts to come in, and then time after that for Harold to repair the damage. Ordinarily, such a delay would have been frustrating, but for some reason, he felt as if he'd been given a reprieve. At least he had a valid excuse for staying on in Call City, instead of passing through as he'd planned.

He glanced up at the sky, gauging the building cloud bank against a possible threat of rain, and then looked around for Charlie's car. When he'd seen her last, she'd been going into the doctor's office with

Rachel. Sure enough, the car was still in the parking lot. He paused, debating with himself about checking in on her first or going on to the police station. Truth be told, his curiosity over the missing banker was starting to grow. But he thought of Charlie, trying to cope with a wiggly baby and a sore ankle, and opted for the doctor's office first.

The street was nearly deserted. A couple of cars were parked two blocks down on his left and there was another in the parking lot beside Charlie's car. An old red hound ambled out of an alley and started across the street, sniffing along the pavement as it went. Several blocks away, a hulking figure of a man was coming up the street toward him, pulling a child's red wagon as he went. Every now and then he would stop and dig through the trash cans at the edge of the curbs, obviously searching for recyclable cans.

Judd grinned to himself. This was a far cry from the big-city atmosphere of Tulsa. He stood for a while, watching the fervor with which the man searched. It was only after he'd come a bit closer that Judd realized the man was quite young, and obviously slow, both in mind and body. The childlike expressions that crossed the man's face were quite touching, and his heart went out to the man-child who would never grow up.

A couple of minutes passed. Finally, the man was only a few yards away.

"Looks like you've got quite a load," Judd said, pointing to the bed of the wagon and the rattling cans.

The man looked up, startled by the presence of a stranger.

The moment Judd spoke, he regretted the impulse. It was obvious the man was frightened.

"My name is Judd Hanna," he said. "I'm staying with Wade and Charlie Franklin. Do you know them?"

The man's face lit, from the inside out. "Rachel," he said, nodding eagerly.

Judd smiled. "Yes, and Rachel," he added. "So, she's charmed even you. What's your name, son?"

"Davie. My name is Davie."

Judd held out his hand. "Hello there, Davie. Pleased to meet you."

Davie hesitated, but only for an instant. He knew about handshakes. He just hadn't been offered one before. He wiped his hand on his shirt and then clasped Judd's hand, giving it a vigorous shake.

Judd noted that the man's clothes were clean, and his hair, while in need of a cut, was definitely not shaggy. Someone was taking good care of him.

"I'm going to work now," Davie announced, and reached for the wagon tongue.

Judd smiled as Davie moved past him. "Good hunting," he said.

But Davie was already focused on more important matters, like the next untested garbage can and the treasure trove of cans that might be waiting.

Judd started across the street to the doctor's office as the sound of rattling cans faded behind him. He entered to the sound of a baby's cry, and to his dismay, saw Rachel in tears with Charlie not far behind. Ignoring the curious stares of the others in the waiting room, he hurried toward them.

"What's wrong with her?" he said, cupping the back of Rachel's head.

Charlie looked up, her eyes filled with sympathetic tears.

"It was time for her last booster shot. She's pretty unhappy with me and the world right now."

"Bless her heart," Judd muttered.

Upon seeing a new and sympathetic face, Rachel set up another howl and held out her hands for Judd to take her.

"Do you mind?" Charlie asked. "I need both hands to write this check."

Judd grinned and lifted the baby out of Charlotte's arms.

"It would be my pleasure," he said. "Come with me, little girl. Let's go see if we can see any birds."

Rachel hiccuped on a sob, hushing almost instantly. "Birds?"

He grinned. "Yeah, punkin. We're going to look for some birds." Then he winked at Charlie. "We'll be outside, scanning the skies."

She smiled gratefully.

"Tweet-tweet," Rachel said, mimicking the bird sound she'd been taught.

Everyone in the waiting room laughed. Rachel didn't know what was so funny, but being the instant center of attention was a lot better than getting a shot. She gave everyone a teary smile and clung to Judd's collar as they started out the door.

"Here, these might help," Charlie said, handing Judd a plastic sandwich bag full of miniature marsh-mallows.

"She likes these?" Judd asked.

Charlie rolled her eyes. "Oh, yes. Just don't let her put them all in her mouth at one time."

"Right," he said, looking a little nervous as Rachel reached for the bag.

A few moments later, they were gone.

''Who was that?'' the receptionist asked as Charlie handed the woman her check.

Charlie glanced out the window. From where she was standing, she could just see the back of Judd's shirt and the top of Rachel's head, but they were both looking toward the sky. She looked back at the receptionist and stifled a smile. Curiosity was eating her up.

''Oh, you mean Judd? He's the man who saved Rachel and me from Tucker's bull.''

Every gaze in the waiting room swerved toward the man outside. They'd already asked about Charlie's limp and learned of their brush with death. But now, to actually see the hero of the moment was too much to ignore.

Then Charlie added, ''Actually, he's a policeman from Tulsa, Oklahoma. He's staying at our place while his vehicle is being repaired, and he's graciously agreed to help Wade with the Shuler case.''

The receptionist gasped, then stood and leaned across the counter for a better look at the man on the lawn outside.

''He sure is good-looking,'' she said.

Instantly on the defensive, Charlie dropped her ballpoint pen into her purse and snapped it shut. She'd endured comments from plenty of people about the fact that Pete Tucker had knocked her up and then left her behind, choosing the rodeo life instead of her. Of course, there were plenty more people who thought that when Pete Tucker broke his neck on that bull, he got no more than what he deserved, but that didn't help Charlie's conscience one bit. There was no denying the truth of it all. She'd let a man get too close and come away burned. There was no way she'd let that happen again.

"I'll call you about Rachel's next appointment when it gets closer to time," Charlie said.

The receptionist had been put neatly in her place and she knew it.

"Sure thing, Charlie. You take care of that ankle now, you hear?"

Charlie nodded and started toward the door. All the way across the room, she felt the people's stares and knew she was being judged yet again.

Once outside, she breathed a slow sigh of relief, then gave herself permission to focus on something besides her sordid past.

Unfortunately, the only thing there to focus on was her child and the man who was holding her. The sight of them together tugged at her heart. It occurred to her then that her life was spiraling out of control.

At that moment, Judd turned and Charlie found herself caught in his stare. A long, silent moment passed, and all she could think was, *Lord, don't do this to me again.*

Chapter 4

Charlie pulled out of the parking lot and onto Main Street, but her attention to driving was being distracted by the man beside her. Judd was sitting sideways in the seat and laughing between mouthfuls of marshmallows that her daughter was poking into his mouth. Every other bite that he took, he made a pretend growl and nipped at her baby fingers, which seemed to Rachel to be the height of hilarity. Charlie sighed. That laugh was so like her daddy's, God rest his sorry soul. Then she turned a corner and began slowing down.

"I need to get a prescription filled," she said, and parked in front of the pharmacy.

"I'd be glad to do it for you," Judd said. "Save you an extra step or two."

She hesitated, then gratefully agreed. "Just tell Judith Dandridge, the pharmacist, to bill Wade at the office."

"Will do," Judd said, then he winked at Rachel. "Be back in a minute, punkin. Don't give Mommy all my marshmallows."

Rachel dropped the sack and held out her hands. "Wanna go."

Judd glanced at Charlie. "I don't mind if you don't," he said.

Charlie hesitated, but only briefly. "I suppose it's okay," she said. "But don't let her talk you into anything. She's had enough sweets, and whatever you do, don't put her down. The last time we were in there, she tipped over an entire rack of condoms. When I bent down to start picking them up, she began poking them in my purse."

Judd threw back his head and laughed. He was still chuckling as he pulled Rachel out of her car seat.

"Come on, kiddo. You sound like my kind of girl."

Charlie handed him the pill bottle to be refilled and managed a smile, but her knuckles were white from gripping the steering wheel too tightly as she watched them disappearing into the pharmacy. The image of a big strong man carrying a tiny child was too touching to be ignored. And the smiles of delight on each of their faces only added to her fears. At that moment, she would have liked nothing better than to sit there and cry. But letting go of her emotions was a luxury she couldn't afford.

God, please take away this feeling. I don't want to want that man.

Then she sighed again and looked toward the street, trying to focus on something besides the lump in her throat. Unfortunately, the near-empty street was a mirror to her own life. Granted, she had a brother who loved and cared for her, and she had her child. There was nothing Charlie loved more than being Rachel's mother. But a valid part of her life was missing. She took care of Wade and Rachel and their home—but there was no one to take care of her. She slept alone and wept alone, and for the most part, considered it her just due. But every now and then, something or someone would come along and remind her of how lonely her life really was. It was those times, like now, when she would have traded almost anything to be held in a man's loving arms.

Had Judd been aware of Charlie's feelings, he would have had an entirely different set of thoughts in his mind. But he was too busy fielding Rachel's chatter and grabbing at her busy little hands to worry about the woman they'd left behind. When he got to the prescription counter, he glanced at the pharmacist's name tag as he set the bottle on the counter and wondered about her stern expression. Dandridge. Not Judith, or Miss or Ms., just Dandridge. She was tall, almost as tall as he, and although she didn't look to be more than forty or so, her thick straight hair was iron-gray with a mannish, military cut. Once, he thought, she would have been considered an attractive woman, but now it was hard to see past the bitterness on her face.

"Ma'am," he said, handing her the empty pill bottle. "Charlotte Franklin wants this refilled, please, and she asked me to tell you to bill it to Wade at his office."

The woman took the bottle, noted the name, then gave Judd a considering stare before looking over his shoulder to the window behind him. Only after she

was satisfied that Charlotte Franklin was truly waiting
outside in the car did she step back.

"What's wrong with Charlie?" she asked. "Why
didn't she come in?"

"She's got a sprained ankle."

Judith nodded, then reached for a bottle on a shelf
behind her.

As they waited, Rachel patted Judd on the cheek.
When he pretended to growl at the little fingers inch-
ing toward his mouth, she giggled.

Judith turned. A faint smile broke the somberness
of her expression.

"Rachel is a sweet baby, but she's a handful."

Judd nodded. "I'm finding that out."

She poured a number of pills into a small tray and
began counting them out.

"Are you kin?"

"No, ma'am. Just passing through."

The smile disappeared almost instantly. "Men have
a way of doing that," she muttered.

Judd arched an eyebrow, but wisely kept his
thoughts to himself. Obviously, this woman wasn't
enamored of the male sex.

A couple of minutes later, she handed him a small
white sack. Then, almost as an afterthought, handed
Rachel a lollipop.

Suddenly shy, Rachel took it, then turned her face
against Judd's neck. Judd froze. The soft baby breaths
against his cheek were almost his undoing. Never in
his life would he have imagined that a female this
small could make him feel so weak. He swallowed
around a knot in his throat and gave the woman a
brief nod.

"Thank you, ma'am."

Clutching her lollipop, Rachel glanced up at the woman and gave her a bashful smile.

"Sank you, ma'am," Rachel echoed.

Judd chuckled, then to his surprise, saw a slow smile finally break the somberness of Judith Dandridge's face.

"Come on, punkin, let's go find Mommy."

"Mommy," Rachel echoed, and clutched tightly at the collar of Judd's shirt as they started for the door.

Charlie thought she was prepared for their return, but when they came out the door and headed for her car, her heart skipped another beat. From his long, sure stride, to the breadth of his chest, Judd Hanna was about as much man as she'd ever seen. And although his face was half-hidden by the brim of his cowboy hat, the sensuous curve to his lower lip was a tease. Would he make love with as much force as he moved through life? Probably. She shuddered, then shoved the thought from her mind.

"Well, that was entertaining," Judd said as he slid into the seat after buckling Rachel back in hers.

Charlie looked startled. "Did Rachel misbehave?"

"I was referring to the pharmacist."

Charlie started the car, but hesitated before putting it in reverse.

"I'm sorry. I didn't think. Judith is a little different. Did she give you a hard time about filling the prescription?"

Judd shrugged. "It wasn't that. I just had the feeling the whole time I was in there that I could have cut my own throat in front of her and she would have stood and watched me die."

"I don't get it," Charlie said.

"I mean, she doesn't much like men."

Charlie put the car in gear. "I can understand how that might happen."

Judd blinked, suddenly reminded of Charlie's history with Rachel's father and decided that the wisest path at the moment was to keep his mouth shut. However, Charlie seemed to be filled with a new curiosity.

"Judd."

"Yeah?"

"Did she say anything about... I mean, what did she say when you asked her to...uh—"

Judd sighed. He suspected what she was trying to say, but until she did, second-guessing her did neither of them any good.

"Just spit it out, Charlotte."

Charlie stopped for a red light and gave Judd a glare.

"All right, fine," she snapped. "Did she act like she thought something was going on between us?"

Judd's gaze raked Charlie from head to toe. It was only after he refocused on her mouth that he spoke.

"You mean, do I think she thinks we're sleeping together?"

Charlie flushed, but nodded.

"Hell if I know," he said softly, careful that Rachel didn't overhear his answer.

Charlie's shoulders slumped. "She probably does. My reputation hasn't been all that good since Pete—"

Judd interrupted angrily. "I think you judge yourself harsher than others judge you."

Charlie glared back. "You don't know what you're talking about," she snapped. "You don't know what it's like to be the butt of everyone's jokes, or to hear a noisy room come to instant silence when you enter."

Judd thought of his childhood and his expression went flat. "Oh, lady, but yes I do. And in ways you can only imagine, so don't start feeling all sorry for yourself. You're not the only one life has kicked in the teeth."

Charlie went pale. Her thoughtless words had obviously struck a nerve, which reminded her she knew virtually nothing about the man except his name.

"Look, I'm sorry, I didn't mean to—"

"Just drop it," he said shortly, then glanced at his watch. "I'll help you with Rachel while you're getting groceries, and then I'd better start making good on my promise to Wade to help out with the Shuler case."

"Of course," Charlie said, and put the car in gear.

Even though she knew separating herself from this man was all for the best, she felt regret, even guilt, that he seemed anxious to leave her presence.

An hour later, Charlie was on her way home and Judd was going through the evidence Wade had collected pertaining to the missing banker.

"Is this all?" Judd asked as he sorted through the half-dozen photos and the pages of notes.

Wade nodded. "Told you I didn't have much to go on."

Judd whistled softly beneath his breath. "This isn't 'much,' this is nothing. No fingerprints, no tracks, no witnesses, no blood, no motive, no ransom note. Lord have mercy, my friend, what you need here is a miracle."

Wade dropped into his chair with a solid thump, his expression as morose as his attitude.

"Like I don't know that," he muttered.

But the facts didn't put Judd off. He had always

liked a challenge. This should make him happy as hell.

He stood and walked to the front windows overlooking the street.

"How about grudges or angry clientele from the bank?"

Wade shook his head. "Raymond has lived here all of his life. He wasn't the most popular person in town, but definitely also on no one's hit list." Then he added, "That I can tell."

Judd nodded. "What did Mrs. Shuler have to say? Did you check her angle? Does she have money troubles? Is there a big life insurance policy against Raymond's life? Maybe she's got someone on the side."

Wade snorted softly. "Betty? She's beside herself. Not only does she care for the sorry so-and-so, she wouldn't want to lose her social standing in the community. As for cheating on him, hell, no. There are no secrets in a town this size. Everyone knows everyone else's business. Being the bank president's wife gives her major clout within the women's circles."

Judd turned around. "So you're saying that Raymond Shuler is every woman's answer to a successful marriage?"

Wade frowned. "No…yes…hell, how do I know. From where I sit, Shuler is almost bald, about twenty pounds overweight and has a tendency to use his power to bend people to his way of thinking." Then he sighed. "But there's no law against being a bully, and to my knowledge, he's never laid a hand on his wife."

"Okay, so that's what you know. Now let's start at the beginning…again. You say Shuler was abducted as he was getting into his car?"

"We think so," Wade said. "He was reported missing, and then we found his car. The driver's-side door was open, the dome light was still on, and the keys were in the ignition. The briefcase he'd had with him at the meeting was on the front seat and there was even a couple of dollars in plain sight in the ashtray. Basically, the only thing missing was Raymond."

"I'm assuming you impounded the car?"

Wade nodded.

"I want to see it."

Wade stood, grinning slightly. "That, I can do."

It was daytime. Raymond could tell that much from the temperature in the hot, airless room. His hip still pained him, but less than it had. He wondered what they'd done to him, and then stifled the thought for a more pertinent concern. It wasn't so much what *had* happened as what *had yet* to come.

The fact that the kidnappers had yet to feed him was another fact against his hope for release. Obviously, they didn't care if he lived or died, and then he remembered they had given him water and, besides the stuff that made him sleep, some sort of antibiotic to offset his injury.

He flinched as something lit on his hip and then began crawling around on his flesh. Moments later, he realized it was only a fly. He flexed a muscle, trying to shoo it away, but the pain of the motion was too great. Moments later, he felt it light again, and it occurred to him then that the fly could, at this very moment, be looking for a nice nasty place to lay some eggs. He thought of the festering wound on his hip and groaned beneath his gag. Dear God, maggots! What if he got maggots in the wound?

He began to moan and thrash, trying to pull himself free from his bonds, but nothing budged. In the midst of his panic, he heard footsteps. He paused, listening intently, trying to decipher the length of stride and any accompanying sounds. When the hinges on the door suddenly squeaked, he flinched. Whoever it was had come back. Was this it? Would they finally let him go—or had they come to kill him?

Inside his mind, he was screaming. Then he smelled something sharp and tangy, like the scent of an orange being squeezed, and felt the familiar prick of a needle. Soon, cognizance began to slide. On the verge of unconsciousness, he heard something familiar—something he'd heard a hundred times before. It buzzed and buzzed in a rapid, repetitive fashion.

He sighed. Everything faded, and the imminent revelation was lost.

A ripple of thunder ripped through the sky, rattling the windows near Judd's bed. His sleep was restless, his dreams filled with places that, in daytime, his mind refused to go. Outside, the darkness of the night was a mirror to the terror he was reliving. Although he was safe and dry inside the Franklin household, his mind had taken him back to the place of his youth where, crouched beneath the cellar steps and hovering in the shadows, he prayed he wouldn't be found. The scent of mold and dirt was thick in his nostrils and the thin fabric of his T-shirt was drenched in sweat born of fear. In the brief ten years of his life, he'd been through more hell than a soldier in war. Through all the fear and hunger—all the pain and suffering at

Joe Hanna's hands—he was like a rat in a maze with no way out.

Outside, the gusting wind from the oncoming storm whipped a tree limb against the house, pulling it across the siding in a teeth-grinding scratch. But in Judd's mind, the sound had become a floorboard suddenly creaking above his head. A shudder racked his body as he held his breath and slid quietly onto the floor.

A distant flash of lightning briefly lit up the Wyoming sky, but he was seeing the pie-slice of light spilling down the stairway from the kitchen into the cellar below.

Outside the Franklin household, a water bucket bumped against the fence post on which it was hanging, caught in the gusty front. But to Judd, it was the thump of footsteps on the stairs just above his head.

A faint wail of distress from Rachel's bedroom suddenly broke the silence within the old farmhouse, only Judd heard the wild shriek of Joe Hanna's voice as he dragged him into the light. He didn't hear Charlie come running down the hall, or see the light come on in Rachel's room. Instead, he groaned audibly and prepared himself for the blows.

It was the sudden silence that yanked him out of the dream. He sat straight up in bed, his heart pounding, his body slick with sweat. His boots were right beside the chair he'd sat in as he'd taken them off. His jeans were on a hanger on the back of the closet door, and his Stetson was on a hook near the window. It took a few moments for reality to surface—for him to realize that he was not in the cellar, and that he hadn't seen his father in more than twenty-five years.

"Son of a bitch," he muttered, and crawled out of bed.

Across the hall, he could hear the soft, soothing timbre of Charlie's voice as she put her baby back to sleep, and one door down, the familiar sound of Wade's intermittent snores. Unwilling to stay in the room with his ghosts, he put on his jeans and then slipped out of his room. He needed some air.

But as he opened the front door and stepped out on the porch, he flinched. A storm was brewing and he hadn't even noticed. He lifted his chin, as if bracing himself for a blow. The unsettled elements fit his mood—dark, stormy, threatening. With a muffled curse, he took several deep breaths and then closed his eyes, willing the memories away.

Charlie sat in the old pine rocker, looking down in the lamp light to the baby asleep in her arms. Whatever had disturbed Rachel's sleep was past. Longing for the comfort of her own bed, Charlie sighed wearily, then stood and laid Rachel down, covering her with her blanket before turning out the light. Giving the room one last glance, she tiptoed out. It was only after she was standing in the hall that she realized Judd's door was ajar. She glanced in. His bed was empty. Thinking he'd probably gone to the bathroom, she started to go back to her own bed when she became aware of a draft on her bare arms and legs. She frowned. Had she left a window open somewhere? If she had, it would surely rain in before morning. The thought of cool sheets and soft pillows drew her, but she stifled the urge and went in search of the open window, instead.

She didn't expect to see the front door wide open,

or the man standing in the dark out on the porch. But the moment she saw him, her heart skipped a beat. There was something about the thrust of his chin and the way he was standing that made her think of a man facing a firing squad, defiant to the end. Her instincts were to go to him, to put her arms around him and take away his pain, but self-preservation kept her motionless. And then he turned. His expression was shadowed, but she could tell by the jerk of his shoulders that he was surprised by her presence.

"Judd?"

He took a step backward.

She moved toward the screen door, pushing it wide as she stepped onto the porch.

"Did Rachel's cries awaken you?"

He didn't answer.

She frowned. "Are you all right?"

Then she saw his face. Her first instinct was to run, her second was to express empathy. The latter won. She took a step forward.

When she moved, he panicked. Her sympathy would be his undoing.

"I'm fine," he said briefly, thankful that his answer stopped her. She was already too close.

Charlie frowned. "If you're sure…"

Judd laughed, but the wind caught the sound and carried it away. She shuddered. Somehow, she didn't think the laugh came from joy.

Judd shoved his hands in his pockets to keep from reaching for her. He needed her to leave—now—before he made a fool of himself.

"Sure? Am I sure? Hell, Charlotte, the only sure thing in this world is that life will kick you in the teeth if you smile."

Charlie gasped. The bitterness in his voice hurt her heart. Not even at her lowest, when she'd known Pete Tucker was never coming back, had she felt as bereft as he sounded. The urge to soothe him was strong. This wasn't the man she'd seen laughing with Rachel over marshmallows, or even the man who had pried too close to her own secrets. This was a man she didn't know.

"Is this about your partner…the one who died?" she asked.

"*This* isn't about anything," he said shortly, and pivoted and stepped off the porch onto the grass. The blades felt cool beneath his bare feet, but he knew better than to go too far. Snakes were night crawlers, and he wasn't looking to add to his troubles by getting bitten.

Charlie hesitated, then followed him off the porch.

He didn't hear her coming, and when her fingers curled around his arm, he jumped, steeling himself to stay calm.

"You shouldn't be out here barefoot," he said.

"Neither should you."

He sighed, then combed a hand through his hair in frustration.

"Look, I couldn't sleep. Thought I'd get a little air, that's all."

The wind was getting stronger now, whipping loose strands of Charlie's hair around her face and neck and plastering her sleep shirt to her body. He tried not to look, but it was impossible to ignore the generous thrust of breast and slender curves beneath the soft fabric.

Charlie glanced up at the sky. A streak of lightning tore through the darkness. Thunder belched. The storm was getting closer. She slid her hand to his wrist, then grabbed his hand and began to tug.

"Please, Judd, come inside. The storm is getting closer."

Her gentleness was his undoing. He shrugged free of her grasp, only to cup her face with his hands. To her credit, she stood her ground.

He moved closer. His need to forget what he'd dreamed was all wrapped up in his desire to lay claim to her, to see if her lips were as soft as they seemed.

"Charlotte, I..."

Her hands suddenly splayed in the middle of his chest. He froze. The storm was closer now; the first drops of rain were just beginning to fall.

"Judd...please," she begged.

He took a deep breath. "Please what?" he whispered.

A shaft of lightning split the night, somewhere between the house and the barn.

"Run!" she cried, then grabbed his hand and bolted for the porch.

He had no option but to follow.

Moments later, they were inside and she was locking the door. Before anything else could be said, Wade was coming up the hall with his boots in his hands.

"What's going on?" he asked, giving them a curious stare.

"Rachel had a bad dream," Charlie said. "She woke Judd up. Didn't you hear her?"

Wade sighed wearily as he dropped down on the sofa to put on his boots.

"Hell, no, I didn't hear anything but that phone ringing in my ear. There's a wreck just off the main highway outside of town that's blocking the road. I'll be back when it's cleaned up.''

"Need any help?" Judd asked.

Wade glanced at Charlie, then shook his head. "No, I'd rather you stayed here with my girls," he said softly, and gave his sister a hug. "Turn on the television and keep track of the weather, honey. This time of year, you never know what it's going to do."

"Okay," she said, and then locked the door after Wade as he left.

Now the house was quiet. Too quiet. Charlie glanced at Judd. He was staring at her. Breath caught in her throat. She lifted her chin, meeting his gaze. He took a step toward her and then stopped as Rachel began to cry in earnest.

"She's afraid of storms," Charlie said, and bolted down the hall, thankful for the interruption.

A few moments later, she came back into the room, carrying Rachel and her blanket, then sat down in Wade's easy chair and began to rock.

And so they sat, staring at the flickering lights from the television screen because it was safer than looking at each other.

Chapter 5

Wilma Self had been born and raised in Call City, and since the death of Francis Belcher more than seventeen years ago, she had been their only librarian. Rain or shine, like the postman, Wilma considered it her duty to open the doors promptly at 8:00 a.m. She was big on duty and short on patience, which could have been part of the reason she'd never been married. Every day except Sunday, she walked the four blocks from her house to the library, using the back entrance. It gave her time to put away her things and smooth down whatever flyaway strands the wind might have tugged from her hairdo. Wilma was also rather fond of coffee, and always started a pot brewing upon arrival, to have with the sweet rolls she would bring from home.

And, as always, after her coffee had been poured and she'd changed the date on the check-out stamp at the front desk, she went to unlock the front door.

She was short and plump, and pushing forty, but her step was light. Moments later, she turned the dead bolt and opened the door. After last night's rain, the day was clear with only a few floating clouds overhead. But it wasn't the sunshine that bugged Wilma's eyes. It was the naked and unconscious man on the steps that set her pulse to hammering. She recognized him at once. It was Raymond, all right. Dirty, and in places, even bloody, but in all his natural glory. She gasped, then pressed her fingers to her lips, torn between the knowledge that she must notify the police and the urge to stare at that which she'd never seen— namely, the male body in naked form. Her face flushed as she fought the urge to lean closer. Moments later, the corners of her mouth turned down in disappointment. After all the fuss, she'd expected so much more. Then Raymond began to stir, and Wilma regained her senses by letting out a scream that carried all the way to the gas station two blocks away on the corner.

The attendant came running out from the garage with a wrench in his hand, ready to do battle. Even from that distance, he could see that Wilma was out of her element. He yelled at the kid pumping gas to call the police, then started running. It would be his first visit to the library in more than twenty-two years.

Wade was on his way out the door when the telephone rang. He paused, knowing that at this time of the morning, it was usually for him. He looked back, watching Charlie's expression as she answered the phone.

"Wade, it's Martha. She sounds hysterical. Can't

make too much of what she's saying other than it's about Raymond Shuler.''

Wade bolted for the phone as Judd entered the kitchen, his hat in hand. Today was to be his first full day on the job and he was surprisingly eager.

"What's up?" he asked.

Charlie shrugged, and then spun to rescue the baby's milk cup before it fell off of her high chair.

"This is Wade. What's up?" Then he frowned and interrupted the caller. "Martha...Martha...listen to me. Take a deep breath and start over."

The daytime dispatcher did as she was told, and in the process accidentally swallowed her chewing gum. After a short coughing spell, she regained her momentum.

"You better get here quick," she said. "Raymond Shuler just turned up on the steps of the library."

Wade's heart skipped a beat. "The hell you say. Is he dead?"

Martha giggled. "No, but he was butt-naked. Wilma Self ain't never gonna be the same." Then she added, "He had some sort of injury to his hip. Oh, and Chief, just thought I would remind you that today is Hershel's wedding, and he ain't gonna be any help to you at all."

Wade sighed. On a good day, the young man who was his deputy caused more problems than he solved. He could only imagine the kid's state of mind today.

"It doesn't matter," he said. "For God's sake, don't call him in. I've already got backup in place until he gets back." Then he added, "Did you send for an ambulance?"

"Yes, sir. One's already on the way from Cheyenne."

"I'm on my way," Wade said, and disconnected. Then he turned to Judd. "Better fasten that Stetson down real tight," he muttered. "Our missing banker just showed up naked on the library steps. Other than some sort of injury to his hip, he seems to be fine."

Charlie grinned. "That I would have loved to see."

"Well, according to Martha, Wilma Self got more than an eyeful. Says she'll never be the same."

Judd stifled a grin as Charlie laughed aloud.

"I'll call you later, sis. If you need anything, just give Martha a buzz. She'll know where to find us."

Charlie nodded, watching as Wade bent down to kiss his niece goodbye.

"Unca Wade," Rachel cried, waving her spoon toward his nose.

"Hey, shortcake, watch where you're waving that thing," Wade said, and removed the spoon from her hand before kissing her cheek. Then he handed back the spoon and tweaked her nose for good measure.

They started to leave when Rachel let out a screech. Everyone stopped, then turned to see what was wrong. Rachel was holding up her arms toward Judd, just as she had the day he'd taken her into the pharmacy with him.

"Wanna go! Wanna go!" she cried.

Judd looked startled while Wade and Charlie stared. He glanced nervously at Charlie, then walked back to where the little girl was sitting.

"Hey, punkin, you can't go with me today, but if you're a good girl for Mommy, when I come back, I'll bring you a surprise."

Rachel frowned. Only a few of Judd's words sank in. One of them was *can't,* the others were *good girl* and *surprise.*

"Surprise," she suddenly stated.

Everyone laughed, which brought forth a wide grin. She giggled, and when Judd bent down to kiss her, she sopped the side of his face with the milky spoon.

"Best kiss I've had all day," Judd said as he straightened.

"Here," Charlie said, handing him a towel to wipe his face. "I don't know whether to thank you for hushing the fit, or give you a lecture for bribing her to be good."

Judd wiped his face and then gave her a slow, studied look.

"She might be little, but she's still female. I didn't do anything to her that I wouldn't have done to you."

Charlie blinked, a little startled by his answer. "Exactly what do you mean by that?"

Judd never broke a smile. "I don't pretend to know diddly about what makes women tick, but I have learned over the years that to get along with one, I have to keep her in a good mood, and honey, if bribery is what gets me off the hook, then consider yourself forewarned."

Wade was grinning from ear to ear.

Charlie was momentarily speechless. The sexual tension between them was growing with every passing day. She'd been sleepless for hours after the episode on the front porch last night, trying to tell herself to leave well enough alone. But her heart kept overriding her head. Now he was playing with her, and she knew it. But unless she chose to reveal her own frustrations to Wade and the rest of the world, she was stumped.

"Oh...you're such a man," she muttered.

At that point, Judd laughed. It was a quiet, secretive

sort of chuckle that held promises only Charlie understood.

"Guilty as charged," he said, and then followed Wade out the door.

Betty Shuler was sobbing profusely when Wade and Judd exited the hospital elevator. Judd's first thought was that the man must have died. They hastened their steps to get to her.

Wade touched the brim of his hat with his forefinger in a gesture of respect, then introduced Judd to Raymond's wife. In spite of her tears, the woman took time to give Judd a curious glance. She'd heard all the gossip about the good-looking stranger staying out at the Franklin place, but she hadn't really believed he was a cop until Wade introduced him as such.

"Oh, Wade, you should see Raymond's poor hip. It's awful…just awful."

Wade frowned. "What's wrong with it? Was he shot?"

She set up another wail and poked a wad of tissues beneath her nose to stem the flow.

"No," she cried. "The doctor said he's been burned."

Judd grabbed a handful of fresh tissues from a box on the table and handed them to her. She took them, nodding gratefully.

"Ma'am, did he know his captors? Has he said anything to you about where he's been?"

She shook her head. "No, and he says he doesn't remember a thing." Then she frowned. "And that…that mark…it will be there forever."

"What mark, ma'am, the burn scar?"

She rolled her eyes. "Not just a scar. A brand. Those horrible people branded my Raymond."

Wade and Judd exchanged looks, then Wade led the woman to a chair and quieted her down while Judd waited. Judd accepted the fact that this was Wade's territory. He would be the one to call the shots.

A few minutes later a doctor emerged from the room across the hall. Wade identified himself, then introduced Judd.

"When can we talk to Raymond?" he asked.

The doctor shrugged. "Other than the fact that he's been sedated, anytime should be fine, as long as he gives his consent."

"Exactly what are his injuries?" Judd asked.

"Dehydration, a few bumps and bruises, and one hell of a sore on his hip."

Wade frowned. "Mrs. Shuler said it was a brand?"

The doctor shook his head. "Damnedest thing I've ever seen. It's the letter *R*…for Raymond, I suppose. But why someone would kidnap a man just to slap a brand on him is beyond me."

"Thanks, Doc. If we have any other questions, we'll let you know."

The doctor shook their hands and walked away, leaving them with the next step in their investigation—to interrogate the victim himself.

Shuler was propped lying on his side, but he was cognizant enough to appreciate the fact that his hands and feet were no longer tied. His injured hip had been cleaned and bandaged, and the stuff they'd given him for pain was making him woozy, but he remembered that he'd been found. What he couldn't figure out was how. The last thing he had remembered was another knockout shot in that filth, and then coming to on the steps of the library. His ears were still ringing from Wilma Self's screams.

He flinched as the door to his room suddenly opened.

"Raymond, it's me, Wade. Feel like talking to me a bit?"

Raymond sighed. The police chief. Thank God.

"Yes, sure," he mumbled.

When Judd moved into Raymond's line of vision, he saw fear in the man's eyes.

"Sir, I'm Detective Judd Hanna, from Oklahoma."

Shuler frowned, trying to compute in his drug-induced mind why a policeman from Oklahoma would be in Wyoming, and then he sighed. He didn't give a damn who was here, as long as they caught the people who'd done this to him.

Wade put his hand on Raymond's arm, making the man focus his attention.

"What can you tell us about your abduction?"

Raymond started to move and then moaned.

"Easy, Mr. Shuler," Judd said. "Is there something I can get for you?"

"A drink of water."

Judd promptly obliged, waiting patiently while the man took several sips.

"That's better," Raymond said. "Thank you."

"Sure thing," Judd said. "Now, as Wade was saying…what do you remember?"

Raymond frowned. "Nothing except a pain in my head and waking up to realize my clothes were gone and I'd been blindfolded and gagged."

"Did you ever hear their voices?" Wade asked.

"No. Not ever. I don't even know how many were involved. All I do know is that after they burned me, someone kept giving me shots that put me to sleep. I ran a fever. Probably from some infection. They gave me something for that, because the fever finally went away."

"Do you know why you were taken?"

Raymond looked a bit startled. "What do you mean? Wasn't it because of a ransom?"

Wade shook his head. "No, sir. We had no contact with them whatsoever."

Raymond paled. "They never asked for anything?"

"No, sir."

"Then why did they turn me loose?"

Wade's expression changed from serious to stunned. "You mean you didn't escape?"

"No," Raymond muttered. "Hell, I couldn't have crawled from here to the door, let alone gotten myself into town."

At this point, Judd interrupted. "Mr. Shuler, I'm going to ask you a question, and I want you to think very hard before you answer."

"Okay," Raymond said.

"Do you have any enemies?"

Shuler snorted, then winced when the motion caused him pain.

"I'm a banker, sir. Of course I have enemies." Then he added, "But none that I think capable of this."

Judd persisted. "Think back. Before you worked at the bank, what did you do?"

Shuler frowned. "I was in college. Before that, I was in high school. My father owned the bank. I came to work straight out of college and took over when he died.''

Wade interrupted. ''Judd, exactly what are you getting at?''

''This was never about money,'' he said.

Both men looked startled, but Raymond was the first to speak.

''I'm sorry, but I'm afraid I don't understand.''

Judd never took his eyes from Shuler's face. ''What happened to you was a case of pure revenge. Whoever took you wanted you scared and miserable, and the brand is so that even after you're well, you will never forget.''

Shuler blanched, while Wade congratulated himself on bringing Hanna into the case. This was an angle he hadn't considered.

''But who?'' Shuler whispered.

Judd leaned closer. ''You tell us, Mr. Shuler. Think back—five, ten, even twenty years. Have you ever done something you weren't proud of? Something that hurt someone else, maybe not physically, but socially or financially? Enacting revenge is a crime of passion, and the public humiliation they wanted you to suffer is all too obvious.''

Shuler looked angry, as if he was insulted by the very notion of what Judd had asked.

''No, of course…'' Suddenly, Shuler froze. His eyes glazed over and his mouth went slack. To Judd's surprise, Shuler looked away. Judd knew without asking that something had occurred to him—something he didn't want to admit.

''What?'' Wade asked. ''Did you think of something that might help?''

"No," Shuler snapped, then closed his eyes. "I need to sleep now."

"Yeah, sure," Wade said. "We'll talk later."

"There's nothing more to tell," Shuler muttered.

Moments later, the two lawmen were standing in the hall with their hats in their hands as Betty Shuler bid them goodbye and went into Raymond's room.

"Well, that wasn't much help," Wade said.

Judd shook his head, then set his Stetson firmly on his head.

"Oh, I don't know about that. If I read the man right, I think he remembered something he'd rather forget."

Wade shrugged. "Maybe so, but that's all we're going to get out of him for now. He'll be released soon. We'll talk with him some more after he comes home." Then he grinned. "And speaking of home, it's time we were heading back. No telling what sort of mischief has been going on in Call City with me out of town."

They headed for the door, their long legs matching strides. As they reached the police cruiser, Judd paused.

"Wade?"

"Yeah?"

"What's it like being the only cop in town?"

Wade grinned. "Busy."

"Did you ever think of working in a larger place? You know...where you would at least have someone to work another shift. From what I can see, you're basically on call twenty-four hours, seven days a week."

Wade nodded. "That's about the size of it, and while a competent deputy or two would be nice, nothing would be worth what I'd lose if I lived somewhere else. Call City suits me, and even more, it suits Charlotte and Rachel. I don't want that baby growing up in the big city and getting lost in the hell that goes on there."

Judd nodded as he got into the car. He reached for the seat belt and then paused.

"I know what you mean, but it seems to me that you've got your own sort of hell going on right now with Shuler."

Wade frowned. "Yeah, you're right. You know, I really appreciate your input on this. I might have thought about that revenge angle somewhere down the road, but not this soon."

"What do you think?" Judd asked.

"I think maybe you've gotten too close to some of old Raymond's skeletons. He sure did turn off the congeniality when you started asking about his past."

Judd nodded. "Maybe when we get back to headquarters, we can do a background check on the man. I have a feeling that your answer is somewhere in Shuler's past."

"Good idea. We better get cracking. I want to find out who was responsible for this. The last thing I need is a repeat performance by the perp."

A few miles down the road, Judd turned to Wade.

"Before we go home tonight, I need to stop by the grocery store and get Rachel's surprise. Even though she's only two, I have a feeling she won't have forgotten it."

Wade gave Judd a considering look.

"She sure has bonded with you, and that's unusual."

"She's a great kid," Judd said.

"Got any of your own?" Wade asked.

Judd's expression went flat. "No, but if I did, I damn sure wouldn't have bailed out on them like that son of a bitch did to Charlie and Rachel."

Judd's indignation on Charlie's behalf was food for thought as Wade continued toward Call City. On the one hand, he liked Judd Hanna, was even learning to trust him. But on the other, he sensed that the man wasn't the kind who would stay in a place as small as Call City, which led him to his next concern. He was beginning to suspect that Judd and Charlie were interested in each other. His sister was a grown woman. He wasn't about to tell her how to live her life.

But…if Judd Hanna hurt Charlie in any way—

He gritted his teeth and kept on driving. No need to borrow trouble. There was always plenty of the real stuff on hand to keep him busy. As for Judd and Charlie, the safest bet would be to wait and see.

Less than an hour before Wade Franklin's normal quitting time, a jailbreak occurred in Cheyenne. According to reports, the three escapees were last seen heading toward Call City and points north. With the help of the state police, a roadblock was set up on the highway in and out of Call City. Once everything was in place, the officers sat down to wait. Judd's surprise for Rachel, a large bag of multicolored miniature marshmallows, lay on the seat beside him. The longer they waited, the more tempted he was to tear into the bag and sample some of them for himself. But he kept picturing her delight and the powdered sugar that would color her smile, and he just leaned back in the seat and stretched his legs, instead. Almost an hour had come and gone before it dawned on Judd that he was actually content. In Tulsa, being static for this length of time would have gotten on his nerves. He put his hands behind his neck and flexed his shoulder muscles, wondering what it was about this place that made it seem different. Was it the slower way of life, or the people themselves?

In the distance, he could just make out the high school band, practicing on the football field. Off to his right, a herd of cattle was grazing near the highway, oblivious to the unfolding drama only a few yards away. A young girl on a bicycle came pedaling down a dissecting street and was quickly turned back by an officer from the state police. It was calm— almost too calm.

He turned his attention toward the highway stretching out in front of him and stared, watching the meager flow of approaching traffic. Already they'd let a couple of eighteen-wheelers through, a farmer with a truckload of hay, and a school bus loaded with junior high football players en route to a neighboring school. There was always the chance that the escapees would take another route, but until they knew for sure, here they sat.

A few minutes later, the silhouette of another eighteen-wheeler appeared on the horizon. At first, he thought little of it, but as he continued to watch it, he began to tense. He pulled himself straight in the seat, then leaned forward over the steering wheel, staring intently at the way the truck was moving. He got out of the cruiser, then a few seconds later, his hand moved to the butt of the handgun he wore on his hip.

"Wade."

Wade Franklin turned from the conversation he'd been having with one of the state police.

"Yeah, what's up?"

Judd nodded toward the truck. It was less than a quarter of a mile from the roadblock with no signs of slowing down. As they watched, a sudden belch of black smoke puffed from the smokestack. The trucker had shifted gears, all right, but up, not down. The truck was bearing down on them with increasing speed.

"Oh, hell, he's gonna run it," he yelled, waving to the officers.

Men scattered, taking cover behind their vehicles as they all pulled their guns, waiting for the order to shoot. Tension continued to build as the roar of the diesel engine filled their ears.

Then suddenly, from behind them, came the persistent squeak of an unoiled wheel. Tin rattled and the men turned in dismay to see the lumbering man-child with his little red wagon, standing in the middle of the highway and staring curiously.

Wade broke free from the group and started waving his hands.

"Run, Davie! Get off the highway."

The men groaned in unison when Davie just waved back.

Wade glanced toward the approaching truck. The engine was wide open now and running hot. He looked back at Davie, then made an instant decision. God willing, he just might make it. "Open fire!" Wade shouted. "I'm going after him."

"Aim for the tires," someone yelled, but Judd knew that if they waited for the truck to reach them, it would be too late—for both Davie and Wade. With-

out thinking of the consequences of his actions, he
darted out from behind his vehicle and began running
toward the truck, moving parallel with the highway.

When the truck was only a couple of hundred yards
ahead, he stopped and took aim. Through the windshield, he could see the figures of three men. The one
by the passenger side of the window suddenly leaned
out, aimed a rifle across the hood of the truck and
fired. Judd flinched at the sound but stood firm. It was
just like qualifying at target practice, only this target
wasn't paper, and if he missed, the consequences
were deadly. Behind him, he could hear the sounds
of men running and knew that some of the other officers had picked up on his plan.

His first shot hit the outside tire on the driver's side,
ripping through the rubber with deadly force. By the
time the tire blew, sending shards of steel-belted
rubber into the air, he had already fired his second
shot into the tire beside it.

Suddenly, the truck swerved, and Judd could see
the three men in the cab scrambling to hang on. As
the cab began to tilt, Judd pivoted quickly, then ran
up the slope of the shoulder toward a nearby fence,
vaulting it with room to spare, before turning and
emptying his gun into the tires on the back axle. Other
officers followed suit, moving in desperation to get
clear of the truck cab that was already on its side and
being pushed against the concrete by the momentum
of the trailer behind it. Moments later, the trailer followed by falling onto its side. The metal surface of
the cab and trailer skidded along the pavement in a
high-pitched scream, sending sparks into the air like
shards from a welder's torch. It hit the first two police
cars in the roadblock, buckling them like empty pop

cans. Men were shouting and running, and the stench of diesel fuel was everywhere.

Judd looked back. The little red wagon was right where Davie had been standing, but Wade and Davie were nowhere in sight. Something popped, and a police cruiser burst into flames. He flinched and dropped, covering his head as burning fuel shot into the air. In the distance, the sound of sirens could be heard, and he knew that someone had called the volunteer fire department.

Seconds later, he raised his head. The truck had stopped. Exhaling slowly, he got to his feet.

"You okay, buddy?"

Judd nodded at a highway patrolman who'd taken cover not far from him.

"Damn, that was something," the patrolman said, and then parted the fence wires for Judd to crawl through. He did so, then returned the favor before they headed for the wreck.

Three police cars, as well as the truck, had been totaled. Smoke was spilling out from beneath the hood of the truck cab as the passenger's-side door began to open. A man looked out.

"Don't shoot," he yelled. "I give up."

"Throw out your weapons," someone yelled.

Two handguns and a rifle were promptly ejected.

"I'm comin' out," the man yelled, then, with effort, managed to pull himself out of the overturned cab before dropping to the pavement below.

Another man followed his lead, dropping to his knees and putting his hands behind his head as soon as he got on the ground.

"Artie's dead," the man said as a state policeman cuffed him.

"Artie should have used his brakes," the policeman said, and escorted him to a waiting patrol car.

Judd squinted his eyes against the blowing smoke and circled the wreck, stepping over fire hoses and looking for Wade at the same time.

Then he saw him, standing at the edge of the highway a short distance away, with his arms around Davie, patting him gently on the back. As he neared the little red wagon, he reached for the tongue, then pulled the wagon along with him. The intermittent squeak of the unoiled wheel seemed almost comical after everything else that had occurred.

At the sound, Davie turned. Judd could tell that he'd been crying. *Poor kid. He must have been scared to death.*

"Davie, here's your wagon, all safe and sound."

Davie grabbed the wagon tongue and then dropped to his knees and began frantically counting the cans inside. Judd squatted down beside him, his heart going out to the man who could not count past the number three.

"They're all there, son. Just like you left them, okay?"

The calm, ordinary tone of Judd's voice seemed to help settle the young man's panic.

"All there?" Davie asked.

The lost, vacant look in Davie's eyes struck an echo in Judd's heart. Davie looked like Judd sometimes felt. But before he could say anything more, they heard a woman screaming Davie's name.

They stood. Only Judd seemed surprised by the woman's appearance. It was the steel-jawed pharmacist, Judith Dandridge.

"Davie! Davie!" she shouted as she raced toward them.

Davie began to get nervous all over again. "My aunt Judy is crying," he said, his voice shaking with every breath.

"She's okay," Wade said. "You just scared her, that's all."

Judith reached them moments later and grabbed Davie by the shoulders in a desperate embrace.

"What happened? What happened?" she cried.

"Some prisoners escaped out of the Cheyenne jail. Davie wandered into the middle of a state police road-block, but he's okay."

Judith paled as she pulled Davie's head down to her shoulders and patted him on the back.

"Davie, darling, you could have been hurt."

"Cans, Aunt Judy. I was lookin' for cans."

Judd watched a muscle jerking at the side of her jaw as she struggled to maintain composure. When they suddenly made eye contact, Judd was struck by how different she appeared now from the woman behind the counter.

"Take him on home," Wade said. "I think he's had enough excitement for one day."

Judith Dandridge nodded, then, taking Davie by the hand, they walked away, accompanied by the rattle and squeak of the little red wagon.

"Damn," Wade said as he watched them walk away. "It's times like these that make me so grateful that Rachel was born healthy and whole."

"So she's his aunt?" Judd asked.

Wade shrugged. "Not really. Judith's parents kept foster children. Davie was the one that never left, so to speak. I think they adopted him when he was around seven, maybe eight. Anyway, her father, Henry Dandridge, owned the pharmacy. After college, she came back to work with him, but when her parents were killed in an accident, she inherited his business...and Davie.''

"Hell of a load," Judd muttered.

"Her shoulders are broad," Wade said, then clapped Judd on the back. "Gutsy move back there, going after the truck like you did. It bought me enough time to get Davie out of harm's way." Then he added, "Let's see what's left to do here. Personally, I've had just about enough of this day."

Judd glanced around, taking note of the fact that the police car he'd been driving had come out of the mess unharmed. He thought of Rachel's marshmallows, and of the little girl waiting back home for her surprise.

"Yeah," Judd said. "Besides, I've got a date with a certain little angel and a bag of marshmallows."

Chapter 6

Wade was quiet on the long drive home, and without the need for constant conversation, Judd had the time to appreciate the sunset from the front seat of the car. Tomorrow, the repairs on his Jeep would be finished, but he wouldn't be leaving—not until Wade's absent deputy got back from his honeymoon. He'd promised. Even though the initial condition of his stay had hinged upon the missing banker who had since turned up, Judd knew he wasn't ready to leave. Using the deputy's honeymoon for an excuse did both him and Wade a favor.

As he watched, a bright streak of orange began appearing across the sky, adding a new layer to the purple-hued clouds on the horizon. He sighed. It would be a long time before the images of this day faded from his mind. From the moment he'd walked into the kitchen and had seen Charlie making breakfast and laughing at her child, to the image of Wade standing at the edge of the highway with his arms around Davie's shoulders, it had been a day like no other. The bag of marshmallows he'd bought for Rachel was on the seat beside him. He picked it up, imagining the baby's delight when he handed it over. An awareness came suddenly, like a fist to the gut, frightening him more than any shootout had ever done. He was letting himself become attached—too damned attached—to Wade Franklin's family. In their eyes, he was just a man passing through. But sometime during the past few days, he'd let himself ignore the fact that he'd be moving on. He stared at the sky, watching until all light was gone and there was nothing to see but the first evening star. A distance ahead, a coyote suddenly ran across the highway in front of Wade's car, momentarily caught in the glare of the headlights, and then it was gone. A loner—just like him.

A few minutes later, Wade began slowing down and Judd noticed that they were almost home. As he looked to his right, the headlights revealed the ruts his tires had left as he had spun out through the bar ditch and then through Wade's fence, trying to beat a bull to a little baby girl. That single action, done without a second thought, had changed his life forever.

Then Wade topped the hill just above the old house. There, shining in the window was a lamp, like a beacon to the lost.

Judd pointed. ''Charlie must be reading to Rachel. The lamp by your easy chair is on.''

Wade chuckled. ''No. That's just a family tradition that Mom started years ago when our father worked away from home. She turned on that lamp every night about dusk, and didn't turn it off until Daddy was home.''

A shiver ran up the back of Judd's neck as he stared at the warmth of that yellow light piercing the surrounding dark.

''You mean Charlie leaves that on for you every night until you're home.''

''Yeah.''

''*Every* night?''

Wade nodded.

A knot formed in the back of Judd's throat. He kept thinking of the years of his childhood, and the countless times he'd come home to a dark and empty house to fend for himself. Not once had he ever known that kind of safety. He glanced at Wade and tried not to covet that which was not his. But as they drove into the yard and then parked, Judd knew he was fighting a losing battle. He got out of the car with the marshmallows in his hand and took a deep breath. In his heart, he suddenly knew this was what had been missing. He wanted to be loved—and missed—and trusted like this. And he wanted it bad.

When Charlie saw the headlights of the approaching car, her heart skipped a beat. They were home! It didn't occur to her until she was moving toward the hall mirror to check her hair that she was doing something she never did for Wade—checking her appearance. Added to that, she was wearing a dress and she'd put up her hair. Ignoring the implications of her own actions, she looked at herself in the mirror, making sure she was still in one piece.

The woman looking back seemed scared—but she also looked more alive than she'd been in years. Just

for a moment, she let herself imagine what it would
be like to welcome Judd Hanna home every night—
to be enfolded within his embrace and feel the
warmth of his breath on her face…just before he
kissed her hello. Angry with herself, she frowned.
This was stupid. She'd played with fire once and had
gotten burned. But Judd Hanna was a far cry from
Pete Tucker. Something told her his fire would con-
sume her. As footsteps sounded on the porch outside,
she bit her lip and then turned away.

"Rachel! Uncle Wade is home!"

A faint squeal, accompanied by the pitter-pat of
stocking feet, sounded up the hall. Moments later, Rachel came into the room, her face wreathed in smiles
as the two men came inside.

Wade grinned and swung her up in his arms, burying his nose in the place below her ear and kissing it
soundly, which sent Rachel into giggles. Charlie
watched, a smile on her face as the familiarity of the
scene played out before her.

But Judd was caught in a very different web—not
Rachel's, but Charlotte's. Then he realized the connotation of what he'd thought and almost grinned.
Charlotte's web. Wasn't that some children's book—
about a pig and a spider? Yes, that was him. Caught
in the web of Charlotte Franklin's love. But what dug
at him most was that the joy on her face was for her
brother and her child, not for him.

So, truth hurts, he reminded himself, but it wasn't
going to kill him. He could still store up the memories
of Charlotte Franklin—from the way her eyes crin-
kled at the corners when she laughed, to the way she
chewed on the lower edge of her lip when she was
trying to be stern.

As he watched her, it occurred to him that her hair looked different tonight. It was the first time he'd seen it up off her neck. It made her look younger, more vulnerable. And she was wearing a dress, instead of her usual T-shirt and jeans. It was made of something yellow that clung to her body as she moved, and he decided that yellow had become his new favorite color. The thrust of her breasts against the fabric was nothing less than a taunt, and he could have spanned her waist with his hands. Her bare arms and neck were a warm, golden tan, as were the sandals she was wearing. He knew, if he moved just the least bit closer, he would smell perfume, as well.

"Sorry we're late," Wade said.

Charlie grinned. "Like this is the first time?" He looked a little guilty, which made Charlie add, "I heard about the roadblock from the dispatcher. I'm just thankful you're both all right."

She glanced at Judd then and smiled, as if finally giving herself permission to look at him, too, when, in fact, she'd been all too aware of him from the moment they'd entered the room.

Judd knew he was staring, but he couldn't make himself stop it.

"Lady, you're sure something to come home to," he said.

Wade looked startled, only then noticing that Charlie was wearing a dress and that her hair was different. Guilt hit him again.

"Yeah, Charlie, you look nice. What's the occasion?"

Charlie could have willingly strangled her brother. "There is no occasion," she muttered. "And I didn't dress up. This dress is at least five years old."

"Maybe so," Judd said. "But it has certainly withstood the test of time."

Then he glanced at Rachel and tweaked a lock of her hair.

"Hey, punkin, I brought your surprise, just like I promised."

When he held out the bag of marshmallows, Rachel squealed with delight and went from Wade's arms to Judd's without a backward look.

Wade arched an eyebrow as his niece abandoned him. "Just like a woman," he drawled, and then laughed. "If my own niece will abandon me for nothing more than a bag of marshmallows, then it's no wonder I'm not married."

Charlie grinned. "We have our priorities," she said, then turned away, ignoring a spurt of jealousy for the fact that her daughter had the luxury of testing Judd Hanna's hugs when she did not. "I kept supper warm," she said. "I'll have it on the table by the time you two wash up."

That night, Judd slept without dreams, secure in the knowledge that for a while, he was safe within these walls in a way that he'd never been before. It wasn't until day was breaking that he roused, and when he did, he lay for a moment, trying to figure out what had wakened him. He cocked his head, listening to the soft scraping sounds in the hallway beyond his door, then the ensuing silence that came afterward. A few seconds later, he heard a distinct thump and then another sound he couldn't decipher. It wasn't Charlie, that much he did know. Over the past few days, he'd learned to distinguish her movements apart from everyone else, like the lightness of her step, the methodical manner in which she prepared all their meals, even the gentleness of her reprimands as she dealt with the messes her baby often made.

As for Wade, he couldn't have been quiet if his life depended on it. He was big and noisy and moved through rooms the way he moved through life. So, Judd thought, that left only one other person who could be making those sounds. Unless there was a burglar in the house, Miss Rachel was up for the day.

He smiled to himself and then rolled out of bed, curious as to what a two-year-old would be bent upon doing at this hour of the morning. He put on his jeans and then slipped into the hall, moving soundless through the house on bare feet. He peeked in the living room, thinking she might have headed for the television, because she'd only recently learned how to turn it on, but she wasn't there. Another thump sounded, this time, accompanied by a small squeak. He spun around. The sound was coming from the kitchen, but when he got there, she was nowhere in sight. Curious as to where she had gone, he stood for a moment, listening.

"Rachel…where are you?" he called.

Total silence.

"Rachel…it's me, Judd."

Still nothing.

A niggle of concern pulled him farther into the room. That was when he noticed that the pantry door was ajar. He turned on the lights, then moved toward it.

She was sitting in the corner of the pantry with her blanket around her neck and the bag of marshmallows in her lap. Already a rim of powdered sugar encircled her lips, and her little chipmunk cheeks were full to overflowing with the mouthful she was trying to chew. She looked up at him and smiled, and as she did, one small syrupy-looking drool slipped out of the corner of her mouth.

For the second time in less than a week, Judd Hanna found himself falling in love. He grinned as he walked inside, then surprised himself, as well as her, by sitting down right beside her.

"Whatcha got, baby girl?"

"'Mallows," Rachel said, talking around the ones already in her mouth.

"Can I have one?" Judd asked.

Pleased that she had an excuse to dig into the sack for more, Rachel crammed her hand into the sack, then poked the tiny marshmallow she pulled out into his mouth.

"Mmm-hmm," Judd said, making a big pretense of smacking his lips and licking her fingers.

As she ducked her head and giggled, another dribble of syrup oozed out of her mouth.

He swiped at it with his thumb, then winked. "Better swallow that bite you've got in there," he said, poking gently on the sides of her cheeks.

She quickly obliged, then before he could stop her, she filled her mouth back up again. It was all he could do not to laugh.

Then to his surprise, Rachel crawled onto his lap, her blanket still around her neck, and continued to dig through the sack, every now and then bestowing him with another bite. Humbled by her trust, he became so focused on watching her that he didn't realize they were no longer alone.

With the instinct of a natural-born mother, Charlie knew without looking that something was amiss with her daughter. Dressing quickly, she slipped out of her room without making a noise, but when she got to Rachel's room, both she and her blanket were gone. Charlie sighed. This new spurt of independence was to be expected, but it was worrisome, just the same. As she started up the hall in search of her daughter, she noticed Judd's door ajar. When she peeked in, she saw that his bed was empty, as well. A bit of her tension eased and she was all the way into the living room before it dawned on her that she was beginning to trust the man—even enough to know that if he and her daughter were together, then that would mean Rachel was safe.

Longing hit her square in the belly, then straight up to her heart. This was getting scary. She didn't know whether to be glad Judd Hanna had awakened her emotions, or worry about what would come next. Either way, it was too late to fret. Awake they were.

A sound came from the vicinity of the kitchen—a soft giggle. Rachel's—she would know it anywhere.

Then an answering chuckle, deep and rumbling. Judd's—she had heard it before, even in her sleep.

She frowned. But what were they doing?

As she stopped at the doorway, she saw them almost immediately, sitting in the shadowy corner of the deep walk-in pantry. She felt like a voyeur. The camaraderie between the pair was impossible to miss. Judd's head was bent to Rachel's tousled curls. His pleasure was obvious, but not nearly as apparent as the joy on her little girl's face.

My baby...she's crossed her first threshold and given her heart to a man.

The moment she stepped into the room, Judd seemed to sense her presence and looked up.

"Uh-oh. Mommy's up. Looks like we've been made."

Rachel fisted the loose edges of the bag as Charlie came toward them.

"Pease?" Rachel said.

Charlie tried to look stern. "Rachel Ann, aren't you asking permission just a little bit late?"

Judd looked almost as nervous as Rachel was acting. "Uh...I heard her and I...then we—"

"Save the excuses for someone who'll believe them," Charlie drawled.

Judd started to get up, when Charlie put her hand on his shoulder.

"Is there room for one more at this table?"

The surprise on Judd's face was impossible to miss, but it was soon followed by a gleam in his eye that made her a little bit nervous.

"Darlin', for you, there'll always be room."

Having set her heart atwitter, he moved his long legs to one side, giving her a place to sit down. To his everlasting delight, she did.

The intimacy of sitting side by side and facing each other in the shadowy closet set a mood neither would have dared to suggest. Even with the baby between them, there was an energy impossible to miss.

"So...what's on the menu?" Charlie asked, a little surprised at her own audacity and trying to make light of what she'd done.

Judd peered over Rachel's shoulder into the bag, and then frowned.

"Well, looks like we have 'mallows. Green 'mallows, pink 'mallows, even white 'mallows." Then he added, "But no dry 'mallows. Today, all our 'mallows are being served with a sauce."

Charlie took one look at the mess on her daughter's face and hands and then threw back her head and laughed. It was a hearty, from-the-belly-first laugh that echoed through the house.

Judd listened to the sound coming out of her mouth as his gaze raked the tender curve of her neck. She looked as if she'd combed her hair with her fingers, and her T-shirt and shorts were quite old, but at that moment, he was certain he'd never seen a more beautiful or sexy woman in his life.

"Hey, what's going on in here?"

They looked up, laughter still on their faces. Wade was standing at the pantry door, staring down in disbelief.

Charlie patted the floor and scooted a little closer to Judd, making room for her brother to come in.

"Breakfast is being served," she said. "This morning, Rachel has chosen 'mallows as the menu of choice. Will you have pink ones or green ones, or are you going to be a purist and stay with the white?"

Wade arched an eyebrow, then grinned. "You're all crazy," he said, then lifted Rachel out of Judd's lap. "Sorry, baby girl, but Uncle Wade needs caffeine, not sugar, to get him awake, and you need a bath. However, we'll settle for a good wash at the sink, okay?"

When the weight of her little body left Judd's lap, he felt oddly bereft, even though it was past time to put an end to their snack. He stood, then reached down and offered Charlie a helping hand. After a moment's hesitation, she took it, trying not to concen-

trate on the way his fingers curled around her hand
and wrist, or the breadth of his bare torso.

At the sink, Wade was chuckling beneath his breath
as he tried to wrench the sack of marshmallows from
Rachel's grasp, but inside the pantry, another sort of
war was in progress.

Charlie was standing now, but Judd refused to let
go of her hand. Charlie bit the edge of her lower lip
and then looked up. There was a faint smudge of
sugar on the side of his cheek, probably from one of
Rachel's indiscreet caresses. Without thinking, she
reached up to wipe it away when Judd grabbed her
hand. For a heart-stopping moment, she was caught.
She saw his nostrils flare as he took a deep breath,
and instinctively, she closed her eyes for the kiss she
knew was coming.

It was brief but tender and Charlie stifled a groan.
Even though it was only a kiss, she'd given away
more than she should.

All too aware of Wade only a short distance away,
Charlie glanced nervously in his direction. To her relief, he hadn't seen a thing.

"Why did you do that?" she whispered.

Judd dropped her hands and then cupped the side
of her face. "Just to see if your kisses were as sweet
as Rachel's."

Her heart fluttered. "And?"

He leaned forward until his breath was just a whis-
per against her face. "Lady, I'm going to be on a
sugar high all day."

"Hey, what are you two doing in there?" Wade
yelled.

"I'm kissing your sister," Judd said. "Do you
mind?"

Charlie gasped, her eyes wide with shock. She didn't want Wade to know—not yet. Not when she wasn't even ready to face what she'd done.

Then Judd turned around, tore a length of paper towel from a roll on the shelf and began methodically picking up the marshmallow remnants on the floor.

Charlie stared at the back of his head in disbelief. How could he be so calm? If he knew Wade like she knew Wade, he should be running out the door about now. She stalked out of the pantry, her head held high, and marched straight past Wade to the refrigerator.

"Scrambled or fried?" she asked, yanking a bowl of eggs from the shelf.

Wade gave her a long, considering look, then dried Rachel's face and hands and set her down on the floor.

"How about scrambled?" he asked. "Sort of fits the mood of the moment, wouldn't you say?"

She ripped a wire whisk from a nearby rack and pointed it at Wade.

"Don't say it!" she muttered. "Just don't say a word."

Judd came out of the pantry, tossed the paper towels and marshmallows into the trash, then went to the sink to wash his hands.

Wade gave him a cool, considering look.

"You are a nervy son of a bitch, aren't you, Hanna?"

Judd looked at them then, judging the embarrassment on Charlie's face against a hint of anger on Wade's.

"Yes, I guess I am," he finally said. "But I learned it the hard way. When I was a kid, no matter what I did, I used to get the hell beat out of me on a regular basis, even though I tried to do everything right. I stayed in school. I didn't complain—not even when there was no food in the house, not even when there was no heat or light. When blood was running out of my ears and nose, I lied to my old man and said it didn't hurt. When he didn't come home for days on end, I pretended I didn't care. But no matter what I did, it wasn't enough. And one day, I realized that the only way I was going to survive was to quit worrying about making him happy and take care of myself.''

The revelation had come out of nowhere, and Charlie wondered how long this had been festering inside of him. Her embarrassment gone, she reached for his arm. When he smiled coldly, she stepped away.

''Sorry, Charlotte. I'll take almost anything from a woman but sympathy.''

She winced but wouldn't back down. ''It's called empathy, Judd Hanna, and do you want your eggs scrambled, too?''

Startled by her gutsy change of subject, he blinked, then took a deep breath, making himself relax.

''Sorry, I don't know where that came from.''

Wade shook his head. ''It's okay.''

''No, it's not okay,'' Judd said. ''It's called abusing your hospitality, and I can promise you it won't happen again.''

He started out of the room when Charlie called him back.

''Judd!''

He stopped, then turned.

''Yeah?''

''Your father...did he ever change?''

A dark look came and went in Judd's eyes. "Don't know. Haven't seen him since the night I threatened to kill him."

Charlie paled. Wade gritted his teeth.

"Damn, Hanna, when was that?"

"When I was ten." Then he glanced at Charlie and made himself smile. "Don't fix any eggs for me. I'm too full of 'mallows."

She bit her lip to keep from crying as he walked out of the room.

"Oh, Wade…"

Wade sighed, then put his arms around Charlie's shoulders.

"We were lucky, weren't we, sis?"

Then they both looked at Rachel, who was playing in a puddle of sunlight on the bare kitchen floor. Suddenly, tears sprang to Charlie's eyes and she picked her daughter up from the floor and hugged her fiercely.

"Mommy loves you s-o-o-o-o much," she said softly, kissing the little freckle below Rachel's left ear.

Rachel giggled.

After Judd's revelation, it was a bittersweet sound.

Chapter 7

Nothing more was said about what had happened in the kitchen, but the truth of it rode between the two men all the way into town. Judd Hanna was a man with baggage, who had obvious designs on a woman with baggage of her own. And while Wade never said it, Judd sensed his judgment just the same. Basically, it came down to one fact. If Judd was any kind of a man at all, he would resolve his own mess instead of adding to Charlie's.

As they neared the outskirts of Call City, Judd finally spoke.

"If you'd drop me off at the garage, I can pick up my Jeep. As soon as I settle up with the mechanic, I'll come to the office. You can tell me where you want me to go from there."

Wade gave him a considering look. "I appreciate the fact that you've agreed to stay on, even though Shuler turned up."

Judd shrugged. "It's no big deal," he said softly. "I had no destination in mind when I got here. I still don't. One place is as good as another. Besides, you still don't know who snatched Shuler, or if it will happen again."

"Don't even say that," Wade muttered, and then he shifted the topic of conversation to something else Judd had just said. "What did you mean by having no destination? Aren't you planning to go back to Tulsa?"

Judd shrugged. "I doubt it. Once something's over, I don't ever go back."

Wade's hands tightened around the steering wheel as he thought of Charlie.

"Don't hurt her," he said as he pulled up to the garage and parked.

Judd opened the door, then paused before getting out. He looked down at the ground, taking absent note of the few blades of grass persistently growing between a crack in the blacktop, then nodded without saying a word. Judd closed the door behind him with a solid thump. Wade watched until he'd gone into the office, then he backed out of the drive and headed for the P.D.

Raymond Shuler was home and healing nicely. The infection in his hip was almost gone and his attitude, at least on the outside, was positive. Friends, neighbors and colleagues came on a regular basis, each wanting to hear all about his ordeal. He was basking in the notoriety of being a five-minute celebrity, but at the same time, was struggling with the shame of being found naked and unconscious on the library steps. Only one other time in his life had he ever been that disoriented—or suffered that much loss of control—and he'd been a senior in high school, only a couple of months away from graduation. To this day, he didn't remember a damn thing about what he'd done, only that he'd started the night by celebrating homecoming at a football game and wound up face-down near a creek the next morning, waking up to a squirrel chattering in the trees overhead and suffering from the worst headache he'd ever had in his life. He'd rolled to his knees and puked up his guts, then crawled to the creek and stuck his head in the water, hoping to alleviate some of the pain. It hadn't worked. But when he'd come up for air, he'd seen something in the water that had given him chills.

It was a shoe. A woman's shoe.

The moment he'd seen it, an image had flashed through his mind of a girl running, and then screaming. At that point, another wave of nausea hit. When it was over, the fleeting bit of memory was gone, too. He'd made his way home, half expecting some girl's daddy to be waiting on his daddy's porch with a shotgun in his hand, but the only one standing on his porch had been his mother. She'd burst into tears upon seeing him, and then he'd been grounded for the rest of that month.

When Monday came, he'd gone to school with a knot in his gut, certain that the proverbial ax had yet to fall. But after a few weeks had passed with no revelations, he had convinced himself nothing had happened, after all.

Now here he was, more than twenty years later, experiencing the same set of symptoms. Only this time, pretending wouldn't make his nightmares go away. Every time he closed his eyes, he felt the darkness closing in around him—then the pain on his hip, then choking on the dust and the filth in which he'd been lying. He was convinced that somewhere beyond the safety of his home, danger still waited. Waited for him to show signs of weakness—waiting for the moment when he would drop his guard once again. Only this time, if they took him again, he wouldn't survive.

So when Betty announced that a deputy wanted to talk to him, his gut knotted. On the one hand, he wanted the perpetrators caught, but on the other, he kept wondering if, in aiding in their capture, he wasn't releasing a Pandora's box of his own.

"Raymond, dear...you remember Mr. Hanna? He was at the hospital with Wade. He's filling in for Hershel Brown while he and Mindy are on their honeymoon."

Raymond gave the big man a nod, then waved toward a chair.

"Yes, I remember. Have a seat, Mr. Hanna. Betty, would you bring Mr. Hanna something cold to drink?"

Judd shook his head. "No thanks, ma'am. Nothing for me." Then he turned to Raymond. "Let's forget the formalities, okay? Call me Judd."

Raymond smiled magnanimously. "Then Judd it is. Do you have any news for me?" he asked.

"No, sir, I'm afraid that I don't. And actually, that's why I'm here. So far, there's nothing to go on except the brand on your hip."

Raymond's face turned a dull, angry red.

"I'd rather you didn't refer to it as a brand."

Judd leaned back and took a small notepad from his shirt pocket.

"I stand corrected," he said softly. "Then we'll call it the wound."

Raymond nodded.

"Okay...the *wound* is shaped like an *R,* is that correct?"

Again, Raymond's face flushed. Judd spoke up before the man could argue.

"Look, Mr. Shuler. I know this is painful. But there's only one way to get at the truth, and that's to tell it like it is. According to the medical report, someone branded your hip with the letter *R,* for Raymond, I assume. From the way it was shaped, your doctor was guessing it had been done with an electric branding iron. Do you remember hearing anything?"

"No," Shuler said shortly.

Judd tried another tack. "Think hard. You were blindfolded the entire time, right?"

Shuler nodded.

"Okay, then maybe there was a scent, or something you felt, that you can remember?"

"No," Raymond said shortly. "Don't you think that if I remembered something, I would have told you?" Then he glanced at Betty. "Dear, I believe I would like a glass of lemonade. Do you mind?"

"No, of course not," she said, and quickly left the room.

Judd watched the man's face, well aware that there was something he wasn't saying, maybe something he didn't want his wife to hear.

"You'll forgive me for asking," Judd said, "but I need to know if there is an angry husband somewhere who might be trying to teach you a lesson?"

Shuler's forehead wrinkled in a frown. "I don't follow."

"Were you having an affair?" Judd asked.

"Hell, no," Shuler spluttered. "I've never cheated on my wife and don't intend to start. She's a good woman. I wouldn't disrespect her that way."

"Sorry," Judd said. "But I had to ask."

Shuler made himself relax. "I know," he said, and gave Judd a weak smile. "It's just hard to accept that you're only asking what dozens of people are probably already thinking." He sighed. "But I swear to you, nothing could be further from the truth."

"What about enemies? As a banker, you must have made some people mad, especially on things like foreclosures."

Shuler shrugged. "Honestly, there haven't been all that many in my years as an officer. However, if you'll call my secretary at the bank, she can give you a list. I'll let her know you'll be coming by to pick it up."

Judd nodded, then made a note to himself to pick it up later. When he looked up, he caught Shuler staring.

"You know, the only stranger to come through this town in years that wasn't just passing through is you," Shuler said.

Judd immediately caught his drift and grinned. "Sorry, Mr. Shuler. But if my facts are correct, I was asleep in Wade Franklin's spare bedroom when you were abducted. Besides, if I was ticked off at someone, they'd know it. Blindfolds and branding irons aren't exactly my style."

Shuler flushed. "It was just a thought," he muttered.

Judd nodded. "And not a bad one, except for one thing."

"What's that?" Shuler asked.

"What happened to you is a case of revenge, pure and simple."

Shuler went still. Judd watched as all the blood suddenly drained from the man's face. Shuler's chin began to quiver, and it was all he could do to speak.

"Revenge?"

"Yes. So if you can think of anything in the next few days that might pertain to those facts, I would say it's to your advantage that you let either Wade or me know. Revenge is an odd emotion. Sometimes the reason for it eats at people for years before they decide to get even."

The tone of Shuler's voice shifted into a higher octave.

"Years?"

Judd nodded. "It wouldn't be the first time," Judd said. Then he stood as Shuler's wife came back into the room. "Well, sir, I'll be going for now. Remember what I told you. If you can think of anything…anything at all, just let us know. In the meantime, you enjoy that lemonade, you hear?"

Charlie parked in front of the police department and got out, then turned and lifted Rachel into her arms. Before she could get to the curb, she heard someone calling her name. When she turned, she saw Davie coming up the street, pulling his wagon and waving wildly. She smiled and waved back, then hugged her baby just a little bit tighter, thanking God that she'd been born healthy and whole. She couldn't remember a time when she hadn't known Davie Dandridge. They were close to the same age, and while he'd long ago outgrown her in size, his grasp of reality was still that of a five- or six-year-old. Some people in town called him names, some looked down upon Judith Dandridge for not putting him away with others of his kind, and then there were those like Charlie who were satisfied to let Davie be. He was what he was. A twenty-something man with the mind of a child.

"Charlie girl, look at my clock!" Davie cried, pointing into the bed of the wagon he'd parked at her feet.

She looked down. As usual, the wagon was half-full of crushed aluminum cans. Davie dug between them, grinning widely as he pulled a man's watch from the bottom.

Charlie's eyes widened. "My goodness, Davie, that's some watch," she said. "May I see it?"

Davie hesitated. "You give it back?" he asked.

"I promise," Charlie said. At that point, Rachel wiggled to be put down. "Just a minute, baby girl," Charlie said. "Let Mommy look at Davie's nice watch."

It was a Rolex. Not something one would expect to *find* on the side of the road. She turned it over, masking a gasp as she read the inscription.

To Raymond with love. Betty.

"Oh, my gosh, it's Mr. Shuler's watch," she muttered.

Davie frowned, then snatched it out of her hand before she realized she'd spoken aloud.

"No!" he said abruptly. "It's Davie's watch now."

He tossed it in the wagon with his cans and started up the street. Charlie hesitated briefly, then bolted into the police department. She had to tell Wade. Only it wasn't Wade that she ran into. It was Judd.

Judd grabbed her by the shoulders to steady her on her feet as they collided at the doorway.

"Whoa there, ladies, what's the rush?"

He ruffled the little girl's hair and wished he could have kissed Charlotte Franklin again, just to ruffle her feathers a bit, too. But he'd promised himself he'd back off from Charlie. Now was no time to change his mind.

"Sorry," Charlie said. "I wasn't watching where I was going. Where's Wade? I need to talk to him fast."

Judd frowned. "I think the dispatcher said he went to pick up Harold down at the co-op."

She groaned. "Oh, no. That will take forever. Harold must be drunk, and he always wants to fight when he's drunk."

"What's wrong?" Judd asked. "Maybe I can help."

She hesitated, but only briefly. "Right! I don't know what I was thinking," she said. "I'm so used to running to Wade for…" Then she grabbed him by the arm and started tugging him toward the street. "Out there. Just now. In Davie Dandridge's wagon with the cans."

Judd stopped. "Calm down. You're not making any sense. Take a deep breath and start over. Now, what's in Davie's wagon that's so important?"

"Raymond Shuler's Rolex watch."

The smile on Judd's face slipped. "You're sure?"

She nodded. "He showed it to me," she said. "It had an inscription on the back from Betty to Raymond."

Judd bolted out onto the street with Charlie right behind him, but the street was deserted. He stood, listening for the squeak of the wagon's wheel, but heard nothing but the engine of a passing car.

"Where did he go?" Judd asked.

Charlie shrugged. "That way," she said.

"Go tell Martha to radio Wade. When he gets back, tell him what you just told me."

She nodded, then stood for a moment, watching as Judd started walking down the street at a rapid pace. By the time he got to the corner of the block, he was running.

Davie was scared. Charlie girl said the watch wasn't his—but he knew better. Finders keepers, losers weepers. It was his watch now. He ducked down the alley between the florist and the barber shop, running as fast as he could. The cans in his wagon were bouncing like popcorn in a pan, up and down, up and down. He reached the end of the alley, turning right and then ducking into the service drive of the beauty salon. A delivery van was just pulling out and he ducked in behind it, afraid to look back, afraid to slow down.

Suddenly, someone called out his name. In panic, he stumbled, falling forward onto the pavement and skinning both his elbows and knees as he braced himself against the fall.

"Davie, Davie, darling, are you all right? Why were you running?"

He looked up. "Aunt Judy...I fell down," he said, and when he saw droplets of blood beginning to ooze through the skin, he started to cry.

Judith Dandridge wrapped the big child in her arms, aching for the pain on his face.

"Yes, sweetheart, I see that," she said. "Come with me. We'll get you cleaned up."

"My wagon," he said, pointing behind him.

She sighed. "Bring it along," she said gently. "We'll put it in the back room of the pharmacy, okay?"

He nodded, then followed along behind her in his pigeon-toed shuffle with the wagon bumping against his heels.

A few minutes later, he was sitting on a stool in the back room. His jeans were rolled up past his knees and he was sucking on a lollipop as his aunt began to doctor his wounds. Every now and then he would wince, and she would stop and blow on the spot until the hurt eased. Only after she was through and the bandages were in place did she resume the questions she'd started.

"Davie...sweetheart...why were you running? Did someone scare you?"

His lower lip trembled. "Yes."

Judith Dandridge's ire rose. She'd spent the better part of her adult life standing between Davie and the world, and the older he got, the harder it was for her to protect him.

"Who?" she asked.

"Charlie girl. She scared me," Davie said, and then poked the sucker back into his mouth.

Judith rocked back on her heels. It was hard to believe that someone as soft-spoken as Charlotte Franklin would be unkind to Davie.

"Are you sure?" she asked.

He nodded vehemently. "Yes, Aunt Judy. I'm sure."

"Exactly what did she do?" Judith asked.

Suddenly, Davie looked away, busying himself with the sucker. Judith's eyes narrowed thoughtfully.

"Davie..."

He sighed. When Aunt Judy got that tone in her voice, he knew he had to mind.

"Yes, ma'am?"

"What was it Charlie did that frightened you?"

Davie's chin jutted mutinously. "Tried to take my clock," he muttered.

Judith stared. "What clock?" she asked.

"Just my clock," he said, then pointed to a spot on his elbow. "It's still bleeding," he said. "See?"

Judith took him gently by the arm. "Davie, you know never to lie to Aunt Judy, right?"

His chin dropped to his chest and his shoulders slumped.

"Yes, ma'am."

"I want to see your clock."

He sighed, then slid off the chair and shuffled to his wagon. Moments later, he pulled the watch out from the cans and handed it to his aunt.

Judith took the watch, looking at it in disbelief, then absently turned it over. Suddenly she went pale.

"Where did you get this?" she hissed, and grabbed Davie by the arm.

He cringed. "I found it, Aunt Judy. I found it."

"Where?"

Confusion colored his expression. "Don't remember."

"You have to give it back," she said. "It's not yours."

"No, Aunt Judy. I found it, now it's mine."

"It has someone else's name on it, Davie. That's how we know it's not yours. Now, you have to come with me. We'll find Wade and ask him to give it back."

Davie sat back down on his stool and started to cry again, only this time it wasn't from the pain of skinned knees and elbows.

"But Aunt Judy, he wasn't using it anymore. You said that…"

Judith Dandridge interrupted. "You know better than to take other people's property and you have to give it back."

"But you…"

"That's enough," she said sharply. "I don't want to hear anything more about the subject. You can't have something that doesn't belong to you."

She took him by the hand and led him toward the front of the store.

Charlie was running up the street, searching alley-ways and doorways for a sign of Judd. Wade had been notified, then she'd left Rachel with Martha, the dispatcher, playing beneath the desk at her feet. If Judd hadn't found Davie by now, she had an idea of where he might be.

Suddenly, she saw Judd step out of the barber shop and look down the street.

"Judd!" she yelled, waving as she started to run.

Judd paused, then waved back, waiting as Charlie started toward him. There was an urgency in her movements, just as there had been the day he'd first seen her, running across the pasture toward certain death.

"What's wrong?" he asked.

"Have you found Davie yet?"

"No."

She exhaled slowly, then took a deep breath. "I'm out of shape," she muttered. "There was a time when I could have run the distance of a football field without breaking a sweat."

"I don't know. Your shape looks pretty good to me," Judd said.

Charlie blinked. Suddenly the conversation had jumped from Davie's whereabouts to something far more personal. She chewed on the edge of her lower lip and then looked away, refusing to acknowledge his taunt.

"I think I know where Davie might be," she said.

Judd's attitude shifted. "Where?"

"The pharmacy with his aunt."

Understanding dawned. "That's right. Judith Dandridge is his aunt, right?"

She shrugged. "Not really, but close enough. Come on. Let's go see if I'm—"

Charlie paused in the middle of her sentence to stare at the pair coming out of the doorway a half a block ahead. Judd turned, following her gaze. It was Judith, and she had Davie by the hand.

"Charlie, I'm glad I found you. We need to clear something up," Judith said. "Davie knows you weren't trying to take his clock, don't you, Davie?"

He ducked his head and nodded.

Judd saw a fleeting expression of pain come and go in Judith's eyes, and then she was all business.

"We're on our way to the police department. Davie found something that doesn't belong to him. He wants to give it back, don't you, Davie?"

Again, Davie nodded, but Judd could tell he was doing it reluctantly. His heart went out to the man, trying to imagine what it must be like to live in an adult's body, expected to cope within the parameters of an adult world, yet not able to understand the rules.

"That's great, son," Judd said quietly, and patted Davie on the back. "Mind if I walk with you?"

Davie gave Judd a nervous glance, but when he saw the smile on Judd's face, his expression lightened. He glanced at Judith.

"Can he, Aunt Judy? Can he walk with us?"

Judith shrugged. "If he wants."

The morose expression on Davie's face lightened considerably, and when Charlie patted him on the arm, he broke into a smile.

"I'm sorry I scared you, Davie. I didn't mean to," Charlie said.

"It's okay, Charlie girl. You can still be my friend."

Tears came to Charlie's eyes. "Thank you, Davie. You are a good friend to have."

Happy that all the earlier turmoil was behind him, Davie impulsively threw his arms around Charlie's neck and gave her a hug.

"Charlie is my friend!"

Judd watched the way Charlotte Franklin hugged the young man, gentling him with her touch as well as her words.

"That's good, Davie," he said softly. "You don't want to lose friends like her."

Again Judd's voice wrapped around Charlie's senses, making her long for something unnamed. When Davie let Charlie go, she had to fight the urge to place her cheek against Judd Hanna's heart and let those strong, able arms hold her close, just as she'd been holding Davie.

A couple of minutes later, they entered the front of the police department, just as Wade came from the back.

"I'd better get Rachel," Charlie said, and headed toward the dispatcher's cubicle where the strident sound of a little girl's chatter was mixing with thumps and laughter.

Judith strode forward, taking the initiative.

"Wade, Davie has something he wants to give you."

Wade stood, waiting for Davie to come forward on his own, but his mind was racing. The dispatcher had told him what had been happening. This was the first clue they'd had regarding Shuler's disappearance. If only Davie was able to remember the details of where he'd found it, it could be the break they'd been waiting for.

"Hello, Davie. Let's see what you found."

Judith took the watch from her pocket and handed it to Davie. With only a slight reluctance, he handed it over.

Wade's eyes widened. It was, indeed, Shuler's watch. Considering it was the only Rolex in town, it wouldn't have been hard to identify. Not only that, but he'd been at the Shuler's anniversary party when Betty had presented it to Raymond. He turned it over, running his thumb across the words engraved upon the back.

"Well, now, this is fine, just fine," he said. "You did a good thing, did you know that, Davie?"

Davie's eyes widened and he grinned. Only a few minutes ago, he'd been in trouble, but now someone was telling him he'd done a good thing. He wasn't sure how, but he liked this much better.

Wade took Davie by the shoulder and led him to a nearby chair.

"Where did you find it?" he asked.

Davie started to look nervous. He glanced at his aunt Judy. She was frowning. That meant he'd done something bad again, only he didn't know what.

"I don't remember," he said, and ducked his head.

Wade sighed, masking his frustration, and came at the questioning from a different angle.

"Could you show us where you found it?"

Davie's lower lip slid forward and he began picking at a button on the front of his shirt.

"He just said he doesn't remember," Judith said. "So how can he show you if he doesn't remember?"

Wade gave Judith a wary glance, wishing he could tell her to take a hike. She was making Davie nervous. Hell, Wade thought. That frown she's wearing could make anyone nervous, even him.

"Was Shuler wearing the watch when he disappeared?" Judd asked.

Wade looked up, a little surprised that he hadn't thought to check that fact himself. If he hadn't been, then where Davie found the watch was moot.

"He was never without it," Wade said. "But I'd better check. Everyone sit tight for a moment while I make a call."

He disappeared into his office, leaving the others to wait.

Davie glanced at Judith Dandridge. "Aunt Judy, am I in trouble again?"

"No," she said shortly. "And I don't see what all

the fuss is about. He found something. He came to give it back.''

"The fuss is all about solving a crime," Judd said.

"What crime?" Judith asked. "I understand no money was exchanged and that Shuler was let go loose without harm."

Judd frowned. "I wouldn't call abduction or branding harmless."

She sniffed. "I suppose, but it's not as if he was disfigured in any way. It was on his butt, for God's sake. If he keeps his pants on, no one will ever know." Then she turned away, as if refusing to discuss the incident any further.

Judd frowned. In his opinion, that last remark was full of innuendos regarding Raymond Shuler's inability to do just that. Shuler had claimed faithfulness to his wife and Judd had believed him. But what if the man was lying? What if there were people in this town who knew something Betty Shuler didn't? He made a mental note to himself to talk to some other people about Shuler's private life. The possibility of an angry husband was still a good theory.

But before he could pursue the thoughts any further, Wade came back into the room.

"Shuler *was* wearing the watch when he was abducted," Wade said. "He's on his way down to the department to identify it."

Judith took Davie by the hand. "We've done our duty. If there's nothing else you need, we'll be going now."

"Wait," Wade said, and then added, "Please."

Judith frowned, ready to argue, and then Rachel came running into the room with Charlie right behind her, and Davie's fears were completely forgotten in his joy at seeing the little girl.

"Rachel! Look, Aunt Judy, it's Rachel!"

He dropped to his knees and hugged Charlie's daughter. Judd watched, amazed at the transformation. The gentleness with which Davie held her was evident. Rachel had a handful of crayons in one hand and a coloring book in the other. She thrust it in Davie's face and grinned.

"Color?"

Immediately, they sprawled on the floor with the coloring book between them.

"Sorry," Charlie said. "I can take her on home if—"

"No, that's fine," Wade said, grinning. "In fact, it's perfect. We needed a diversion."

Judith Dandridge's ire disappeared as she stared at the backs of the two children's heads. The fact that almost twenty years separated them in age was moot, because their delight was still the same. She drew a deep breath and then looked away.

But Judd was watching her, trying to imagine the strength of character it would take to care for someone who would forever be a child—especially when it was not a child of your own. His estimation of the woman rose. Obviously, her attention to Davie ran far deeper than duty. Despite the fact that he'd been her parents' foster child, in her own way, Judith Dandridge had come to love him.

Chapter 8

Raymond Shuler entered the police department, walking with the aid of a cane. His limp was pronounced and so was the frown on his face. Everyone scattered to make room for his entrance, including Charlie, who scooped Rachel off the floor, and Davie, who ran to stand behind Judith.

"What's this about finding my watch?" he announced.

Wade held it out. "This is just a formality, but I need you to identify this for me."

Shuler all but snatched it from Wade's fingers, then turned it over. His face reddened as he spoke in an accusatory tone.

"It's mine, all right! Where did you find it?"

Wade pointed to Davie. "He found it," Wade said. "He and Judith just turned it in."

Raymond's gaze scanned past Davie as if he didn't exist.

"Where did you find it?" he asked.

Judith frowned. "I didn't, Davie did. It's him you'll be needing to thank."

Raymond looked flustered, obviously resenting the fact that he'd committed a social faux pas. He stared at the lumbering man-child standing beside her and tried not to let his true feelings show.

"Yes…well…thank you for finding my watch."

The man's angry voice seemed frightening. Davie turned his face against his aunt Judy's shoulder and refused to look at him.

Raymond flushed, taking Davie's behavior as a personal affront, and started to leave, muttering beneath his breath that people like him should be put away.

Judd heard just enough of what Shuler said to get mad.

"I suppose it's a damn good thing he wasn't or you wouldn't be standing there with that watch in your hand."

Shuler glared at Judd, but Judd held his ground. Finally Shuler relented.

"Yes…well, I apologize. I didn't mean to speak out of turn, but this hasn't been a good week for me, you know."

Judith drew herself up to her full height of nearly six feet and took Davie by the hand.

"If you think your life is tough," she snapped, "try walking a mile or two in Davie's shoes." Then she headed for the door.

Judd felt bad, both for Judith and for Davie, who had started to cry.

"Hey, there," he said, patting Davie on the back. "You weren't going to leave without your reward, now, were you?"

Davie blinked. He wasn't sure what that meant, but the man's voice was nice.

Judd took off his own watch and then slipped it onto Davie's wrist.

"How's that?" he asked. "Does it fit okay?"

Davie smiled widely and quickly lifted the watch to his ear to listen for the tick.

Judith Dandridge sighed. "That wasn't necessary, Mr. Hanna."

Judd shook his head. "I disagree. I think it was very important that Davie be rewarded for his honesty."

Raymond Shuler realized too late that the offer should have come from him. He reached for his pocket and pulled out his wallet in haste.

"Yes, of course," he said, thrusting two twenty-dollar bills in Judith's face. "Here, buy the boy something nice."

Judith backed up from the money as if Raymond had tried to hand her filth.

"That's what's wrong with you, Raymond Shuler. You always did think that money could buy anything, including a good reputation."

Then she turned and walked away, taking Davie with her.

Shuler flushed angrily, then stuffed the money back in his wallet.

"Damned woman," he muttered. "She's always been a cold bitch. It's no wonder she never married."

"Known her long, have you?" Judd asked.

Shuler snorted beneath his breath. "We were in school together," he said. "Always thought she was better than everybody else." Then he patted his pocket, making sure his watch was still there, and nodded to Wade. "I don't suppose that retard could help you any with my case?"

Wade flushed angrily, but held his temper. "Davie didn't remember where he'd found the watch, if that's what you're asking."

"Figures," Shuler muttered. "Well, I'll be getting on home now. I'm not supposed to overdo it, you know."

"Wait a minute, Raymond," Wade said. "Technically, your watch is evidence. I need to keep it in—"

"Whatever for?" Shuler snapped. "You're never going to find who did it."

Judd jumped on the comment before Shuler could leave. "Why do you say that, Mr. Shuler? Do you know something we don't?"

Shuler pointed his cane at Judd with an angry jerk.

"I don't like what you're insinuating, mister."

Judd refused to comment, leaving Raymond to think what he chose. A few moments later, he stomped out of the office, leaving a wake of anger behind.

The moment the door slammed behind him, Wade pivoted and threw his keys across the room where they hit the wall with a splat.

"Sometimes this job is hell, and keeping my opinions to myself, even harder. That son of a bitch. Whoever took him should have branded him with an *A* for asshole, not *R* for Raymond."

Charlie was at the window, watching the banker making his way across the street toward his car. Calmly, she turned, giving the two men a cool glance.

"In my opinion, they could have gone either way and still been right. The two are synonymous with

Shuler. As for changing the brands, that would have been stating the obvious all over again. Raymond—asshole. Asshole—Raymond.''

Judd pivoted suddenly, staring at Wade and Charlie in disbelief.

''Well, I'll be damned.''

''What?'' they both echoed.

Judd pivoted and headed toward the file of notes he'd laid on his desk.

''What she said. Maybe that's what we've been missing.''

''I don't get it,'' Wade said.

But Charlie immediately tuned in.

''I think I do,'' she said. ''What Judd's saying is that we've never considered the fact that the *R* on Raymond's backside might stand for something else.''

Judd grinned, pleased that she'd caught on so quickly.

''You're good,'' he said. ''Maybe Wade should have hired you for a detective and sent me on my way.''

''No way,'' Charlie said. ''Now, I'm going to take my daughter and myself home and leave you two to your work.''

''See you this evening, sis,'' Wade said, and gave Rachel a quick kiss. ''Judd, we need to talk. Wait here while I tell Martha we're leaving.''

He left, leaving Charlie and Judd momentarily alone. Rachel was almost asleep on Charlie's shoulder, and when Charlie turned, the afternoon sunlight caught in the curls on the little girl's head.

''Damn,'' Judd whispered, unaware that he'd spoken aloud until Charlie stopped and turned.

"What?" she asked.

He just shook his head and then reached out and touched their heads—first one, then the other—lightly palming some of Rachel's curls before running his hand over the sleek ponytail Charlie had made of her hair.

Charlie's heart skipped a beat. At that moment, if she hadn't been holding Rachel, she would have hurled herself into this man's arms and damned the consequences later.

"Why did you do that?" she asked.

There was a knot in his throat that made his voice tremble.

"Just then...you and your baby...standing in that sunlight." He tried to smile, but it wouldn't come. "You look like a painting I once saw. I think it was called *Madonna with Child*."

Charlie's breath caught at the back of her throat.

"Oh, Judd, I—"

He put a finger across the curve of her lips.

"Don't."

Charlie closed her eyes, absorbing the feel of his hand on her mouth, then she inhaled slowly, masking a moan.

The abrupt tap of Wade's boot heels on the floor signaled his return. They turned away. Judd pretended great interest in the papers he'd picked up, and Charlie readjusted her hold on Rachel as she started toward the door.

"Okay, I'm ready," Wade said.

Charlie was halfway across the room when Judd noticed the way she was walking.

"Charlie!"

She turned.

"You're limping again."

She shrugged. "It's just been a long day."

"Here," Judd said, taking the sleeping baby out of Charlie's arms. "At least let me carry her to the car for you."

As they passed the baby, their gazes met, then momentarily held. Judd could see his own reflection in the pupils of her eyes, and the image of his own vulnerability was startling. Then he gritted his teeth and settled Rachel upon his shoulder.

"Lead the way, Charlotte. It's time to get this little curly-head home."

Long after Charlie was home and had put Rachel down for her nap, she kept thinking about the gentleness of Judd's hand on her hair, then the pressure of his finger upon her mouth. But no matter how hard she tried, the images wouldn't go away. She knew what was happening and it scared her to death. She was falling in love with Judd Hanna.

Raymond Shuler watched his wife leaving for her afternoon club meeting, then turned away from the window and hobbled to the door, making certain she'd locked it behind her. He was tired, so tired, but there was no way he was going to lie down until he was sure that he was safely locked in.

A few minutes later, he made it to the bedroom and stretched out on their bed, careful not to put pressure on the healing wound on his hip. As he closed his eyes, the events of the afternoon began to replay in his mind, from receiving the phone call about his watch, to the dressing-down that he'd received from that uppity stranger Wade had taken into his office. What was his name? Oh yes, Hanna. Judd Hanna.

Raymond frowned. He didn't like the way Hanna had talked down to him, and first thing the next morning he was going to give Wade Franklin a piece of his mind. After all, he'd been part of the city council who'd voted to hire Franklin. He could be fired just as well.

A slight breeze was moving the limbs of one of Betty's shrubs up against the house. The scratch, scratch, scratch reminded him of the sound his fingernails had made as he'd clawed against the hard earthen floor. He shuddered, then carefully rolled over onto his belly, pillowing his cheek against his hand. In another part of the house, Betty's grandfather clock chimed the half hour. It was half past three.

His thoughts drifted, scattering like seeds in the wind, when suddenly, something clicked in his subconscious. His eyes popped open and he rolled abruptly, ignoring the pain on his backside as he reached for the phone. His hands were shaking with excitement as he dialed the police department.

"Call City P.D., how can I help you?"

"Martha, this is Raymond! I need to speak to Wade immediately."

"Sorry, Raymond, but he's out of the office."

"Then do whatever it is you do to contact him and tell him to get to my house right now! This is an emergency! I just remembered something about the people who kidnapped me!"

Martha gasped. "Yes, sir! I'll radio him now."

Raymond hung up, then leaned against the headboard of his bed, weak and shaking. He'd been so certain there was nothing to remember. Now he wondered what else might come as time passed.

Less than five minutes later, he heard a car stop abruptly in front of his house. With a groan, he dragged himself up from the side of the bed and hobbled to the door. He was turning the lock as Wade banged on the door.

"Raymond! This is Wade! Open up!"

He pulled the door wide, his gestures jerky with excitement.

"Come in, come in," he said.

Judd moved in behind Wade, surprised by the change in the man's demeanor. Earlier, Shuler had been nothing short of hateful, and now he was almost ebullient in his greeting.

"What's up?" Wade asked. "Martha said it was an emergency."

Raymond waved them toward the living room.

"Sit, sit," he ordered. "I have news regarding my captors."

Judd stopped and turned, his eyes narrowing. "Has someone contacted you?"

Shuler frowned. "No. Why would they contact me now when they've already let me go?"

"I don't know," Judd said softly. "You tell me."

Shuler frowned. Again, this man seemed to be insinuating things about him he didn't appreciate.

"What I will tell you," Raymond said, "is that I remembered something that happened while I was being held captive."

"Like what?" Wade asked.

"A pager! I heard the sound of a pager going off, and when they moved past me, I smelled oranges."

Wade's expression fell. "Is that all?" he asked.

Shuler glared. "What do you mean, is that all? Isn't that enough to get you started in a positive direction?"

Wade sighed. "Look, Raymond, as you said earlier, you've had a rough week. But you've got to be serious for a minute. Do you know how many people in this town carry pagers? Besides half the kids in high school, the vet does, the mayor does, all of the city employees carry them. I think both pharmacists carry them, and for that matter, I have one, too, and I damn sure didn't snatch you."

Shuler dropped onto the couch with a thud, only afterward remembering his sore backside, but by that time it was too late to ward off the pain.

"Damn!" he moaned, then leaned over on his good hip and put his head in his hands. "What about the scent of oranges?" he muttered.

"Maybe your captor is a fruit freak."

He looked up, his expression filled with disgust. "That isn't funny."

Wade's lips twitched. "Sorry, Raymond, but what else can I say? It's not against the law to eat oranges, and I'd hate to have to sort through the people who've bought oranges at the supermarket over the past few weeks, trying to find a kidnapper."

"It might not even be oranges you smelled, but just the scent of orange, instead," Judd said. "You know...like lemon-scented furniture polish, coconut-scented tanning lotion, peppermint-scented toothpaste—you get the picture."

"Get out!" Shuler muttered, dragging himself to his feet.

"Now, Raymond, there's no need getting mad at us," Wade said. "Look on the positive side of this.

If you remembered this much, there could be even more. Maybe some of it will be more helpful.''

"Just get out!" Shuler said. "No one is taking this seriously. Everyone is laughing at me because I've got a sore on my ass. They weren't scared half out of their minds, thinking they were going to die. They didn't think they'd never see their family again."

Judd's sympathy for the man overrode his earlier disgust as he put a hand on Raymond's shoulder.

"Look, Mr. Shuler, I know this has been tough on you. Have you considered counseling? It might help to talk to a—"

"Oh, sure, that's just what I need," Raymond drawled. "Do you know how many people would withdraw their money from my bank if they thought their president was seeing a shrink?"

"I think you're exaggerating," Judd said. "And I don't think you're giving your friends the benefit of the doubt."

"I don't have any friends!" Raymond shouted.

"Now, Raymond. You know better than that," Wade said. "Why, there were dozens of people who came to see you after you got home from the hospital."

"They were snooping, that's all, just snooping," he cried. "They aren't really my friends. If they were, they wouldn't be making jokes about what happened to me."

Judd glanced at Wade and shrugged. "If what you say is so, Mr. Shuler, then have you ever asked yourself why?"

Shuler blanched. "Why what?"

"Why do you believe you have no friends? Have you treated that many people unfairly? Have you cheated someone enough to make them seek retribution?"

Shuler leaned forward, then buried his face in his hands, his earlier outburst forgotten.

"I don't know," he moaned. "I honestly don't know." When he looked up, his expression was haggard. "The entire time I was tied up, I kept trying to think who hated me enough to do that, but a face wouldn't come. Sure, I've been tough on some of the bank's customers, but I have to. It's my job to protect the interests of the depositors."

Judd glanced at Wade, silently asking permission to continue his interrogation. Wade nodded.

Judd slid onto the couch beside Shuler, waiting until he was calm enough to listen.

"Mr. Shuler, I'm going to ask you a personal question, and I want you to think very hard about it and then tell me the truth, no matter what."

Raymond sighed and then nodded.

"Do you really want these people caught?"

Raymond jerked, then looked up, stunned by the question. Not because he was insulted, but because he'd asked himself the very same question more than once. He glanced away, studying the pattern on the carpet as he tried to find a way to answer without making himself look guilty. Finally, he folded his hands in his lap and met Judd's gaze.

"Honestly…I don't know." Then he added, lest he be misunderstood, "It's not that I liked what they did, but they did let me go. I *am* home." He hesitated, then continued. "I don't know if you can understand this or not, but I have the strangest feeling that if I ever find out, my life will never be the same."

Judd put a hand on Raymond's shoulder. "That's

just it, Mr. Shuler. Maybe you have yet to accept it, but your life has already changed."

Raymond's shoulders slumped. "What do you want me to do?"

"Tell us the truth," Judd said.

"But I did," he argued.

"Then why do I keep getting the feeling that there's something in your past that might pertain to this incident—something that maybe no one knows?"

Shuler blanched. Hanna was beginning to frighten him. It was as if the man saw past all of his defenses to the weak, scared creature beneath.

"I don't know what you're talking about," he muttered.

Judd sighed. "As the saying goes, It's your funeral." Then he stood. "I'm through here, Wade. Unless you have something else you wanted to ask Mr. Shuler, I think our business is done."

"Nope," Wade said. "Don't get up, Raymond. We'll let ourselves out."

"Be sure and lock the door," Raymond said, hating the panic in his voice.

Judd paused and looked back. "One more question, Mr. Shuler."

Raymond flinched. "Yes?"

"This is a small town. You've lived here all your life. Before you were abducted…did you always lock your front door?"

Raymond's mouth went slack. Silently, he shook his head no.

"Like I said…your life has already changed. What if next time, they take your wife instead of you? Are you going to be willing to forget it then?"

Raymond's heart skipped a beat, and when the

sound of the lock suddenly sounded in the silence they'd left behind, he covered his face and burst into tears.

The house still smelled of fried chicken, although they'd already eaten and cleaned up the kitchen more than two hours ago. Wade was down at the barn, checking on a cow that was due to give birth, and Charlie was taking a load of towels out of the dryer. Judd was lying on the living room carpet on his stomach while Rachel climbed on and off of him, as if he were a playground toy. Fresh from her bath and dragging her blanket, she smelled like toothpaste and powder, but her little elbows and knees were beginning to take their toll. He grunted as she walked up the middle of his back and then sat down across his backside as if it were a saddle. When her heels dug into his sides, he pretended to buck.

She giggled, then stretched out along the length of his back and pulled her blanket up over them both.

Judd stilled, listening to her baby mutterings, waiting for her to make the next move. But she didn't. He didn't know when he realized that she'd gone to sleep, but once he had, it would have taken an army to make him move. He felt humbled by the little girl's trust, and wished that her mother was as easy to reach.

He heard her sigh, then felt her fisting a part of his shirt, subconsciously anchoring herself to his back. Judd smiled. He was tired, but it was a good tired. Charlie was bound to come back into the living room pretty soon. All he had to do was wait until she came looking for Rachel.

The steady hum of the air conditioner was hypnotizing. He took a slow breath, careful not to disturb Rachel's rest, and then closed his eyes.

Charlie put the last of the towels on the shelf in the linen closet, then shut the door. Only after she peeked into Rachel's room did she realize that the little imp had crawled out of her bed again. She turned, intending to call Rachel's name, when the silence of the house overwhelmed her. She glanced toward the windows. It was already dark. Rachel was afraid of the dark, so she wouldn't have gone outside. And then she reminded herself, when it came to Rachel, there was always a first time for everything.

She started through the house, checking room by room, telling herself she was making a big deal out of nothing. More than likely, the little imp had snuck back into the pantry for more 'mallows. But then she entered the living room and froze, unable to believe her eyes.

Judd was on the floor asleep, his cheek pillowed by his hands, while Rachel lay asleep on his back, her precious blanket covering them both.

"Sweet Lord," she whispered, and reached for the wall behind her for support. Then she moved slowly, dropping into a nearby chair, unable to take her eyes from their faces. Judd looked more vulnerable, even younger, in his sleep. There was a slight frown right between his eyebrows, and Charlie wanted to kneel down beside him and smooth it away. Rachel's mouth suddenly pursed and then made sucking noises. When Rachel put her thumb in her mouth, Charlie sighed. If thumb-sucking would make her life easier, she might consider it herself. She leaned back in the recliner, careful not to make any noise, then sat without moving, watching them as they slept.

Some time later, Wade came in the back door and went straight to the sink to wash up. It wasn't until he was reaching for a towel to dry off that the unnatural quiet of the house suddenly dawned.

Frowning, he tossed the towel on the cabinet and stalked through the house, only to come to an abrupt halt as he reached the living room. He didn't know what struck him first. The image of Judd and Rachel, both asleep on the floor, or the look on Charlotte's face as she sat watching them sleep. He took a deep breath as a knot formed in his belly. If he wasn't mistaken, his sister was in love, and with a man they knew precious little about.

Chapter 9

The loss of warmth on Judd's back was the first inclination he had that the baby was gone. Blinking sleepily, he raised his head and saw Wade carrying Rachel out of the room. He groaned, then rolled over and stretched. It wasn't until he started to sit up that he realized he wasn't alone in the room. Charlotte was sitting in the chair by the window. His pulse skipped a beat. How long had she been sitting there?

"Charlie…"

"You are a dangerous man, Judd Hanna."

He frowned. "What do you mean?"

Her chin was quivering, and there was a brightness to her eyes that looked suspiciously like tears.

"My daughter has fallen for you, I think. It makes me worry how she'll react when you leave us."

If he stood up, he was afraid she would bolt and run, so he turned to face her instead.

"What about her mother?" he asked softly. "Is she

going to care, too, or is she going to be glad to see the back of my head?''

Charlie stood abruptly. ''This isn't a game. Playing with people's feelings isn't funny, Judd.''

He got to his feet and walked toward her, stopping only inches from where she stood.

''You don't see me laughing, do you?''

Charlie tilted her head, staring intently into his eyes, trying to interpret what was going on behind that dark, secretive gaze. Finally, she shook her head and then sighed.

''I don't know what I see, but I know, as sure as my own name, that you're going to make both of us cry.''

Judd winced. The thought was obscene. He shook his head and then cupped the side of her cheek with his hand.

''No, honey, I wouldn't do that to you—to either of you.''

''Oh, but you will—the day you pack up and leave.''

Angry with herself for giving away so much of her feelings, Charlie ducked her head as she stood, then started to leave when Judd grabbed her arm.

''Wait,'' he pleaded.

She paused.

''I don't know what to say,'' he said softly. ''I've never mattered to anyone before in my life.''

At that moment, Charlie saw past the man to the little boy he'd been, waiting in the dark for his father to beat him. She knew what she felt, but telling him the truth would be giving him even more ammunition with which to break her heart. And yet lying to him now, at his most vulnerable, was impossible.

"You don't have to say anything," she said. "Just know that your absence will leave a very painful hole in our lives."

Then she walked away, leaving him to digest what she'd said.

Only Judd's mind wasn't processing anything past the fact that when he left, Charlotte Franklin would cry. Something inside of him started to give way—something old, and scarred, something ugly that he'd kept hidden. He took a deep, shaky breath and headed for the porch. At the least, he needed some air.

A few minutes later, he found himself at the far end of the corrals and looking back toward the house. At first, all he could see was the dim outline of the rooftop and the faint glow of lights showing through the kitchen and bedroom curtains. Then one by one, the lights in the house went out, leaving it in total darkness. He shoved his hands in his pockets, letting the vast emptiness of the land envelop him.

Off to his right was the pasture where Tucker's bull had trespassed. It seemed like a lifetime ago since the incident, and yet barely a week had passed. Seven days ago he'd been running away from everything he'd known, rather than face the truth about himself. Now here he was, faced with a truth older than time, and he felt himself withdrawing even further. How could he let himself love Charlotte Franklin when he didn't know how to love himself?

His shoulders slumped as he turned back toward the house, and as he did, he saw something that stopped him cold. There was a light in the living room window, burning bright against the night. It took him a moment to accept what it meant, and when he finally did, he felt a lump forming at the back of his throat. What was it Wade had said about that lamp? Something about the lady of the house always leaving it burning until all those she loved had come home?

Wade Franklin was in bed, so that left only one other man for whom that light burned. He swiped a hand across his eyes, angry for the sudden shift of tears.

"Oh, God, Charlotte, don't love me like this."

But she wasn't there to argue, and he had nothing left to say to himself. A few minutes later, he entered the house, pausing to lock the front door behind him. He started toward his room and then paused and went back, turning out the light that she'd left burning for him. Later, as he was drifting off to sleep, the image of that lamp in the window moved across his mind, lingering long enough to give his heart ease. And he slept.

Just after midnight, the phone beside Wade's bed started to ring. Trained to wake up at a moment's notice, he answered before he even opened his eyes.

"This is Franklin," he mumbled.

"Wade, this is Della."

The voice of the night dispatcher at the police department was enough to drag him the rest of the way awake. He sat up.

"What's up?"

"Sorry to wake you, but I think you need to come in. There's a federal marshall here wanting to use our jail for the night, and with Hershel on his honeymoon, we don't have a jailer on duty."

"Tell him to hang tight. I'll be right there," Wade said, then hung up and reached for his pants.

A couple of minutes later he exited his room, carrying his boots. His service revolver was on a shelf in the hallway. As he stopped to retrieve it, he heard a door open behind him. He looked back. It was Judd.

"Trouble?" Judd asked.

"No, I just have to play jailer tonight. Tell Charlie I'll call in the morning."

Judd frowned. "I could do that for you," he said.

Wade gave him a cool look. "Want to explain to a federal marshal why you're pretty much AWOL from your own department?"

Judd grinned wryly. "Not really."

"That's what I thought," Wade said. "It's no big deal, and it's not like I haven't done this before. There's a cot in the office. I'll be fine."

"Okay, but if you need me…"

Wade nodded. "I'll know where you are."

Judd walked him to the door, then locked it behind Wade. He stood, listening until the sound of Wade's cruiser was no longer evident. Then he reached down and turned on the old family lamp, smiling to himself as he turned to go. But the smile died on his face, leaving him weak-kneed and suddenly breathless.

Charlie was standing in the shadows, and even though her nightgown was decent enough, the vague outline of her body beneath the soft, worn fabric made him ache for what she could offer.

"I didn't see you," he muttered.

"Where was Wade going?" she asked, ignoring his remark.

"Said something about having to play jailer for some federal marshal."

She sighed. "He needs more help," she said. Then she glanced at the lamp. "So you know," she said softly.

"Wade mentioned the family tradition the other day."

She nodded and looked away, rubbing her hands against her arms, as if she were suddenly chilled.

"Charlotte."

She looked up, drawn by something in the tone of his voice.

"What?"

"Thank you."

"For what?" she asked.

"For leaving that light on for me."

She sighed, as if giving up some internal struggle.

"You're welcome," she said softly.

He started toward her, and to her credit, she stood her ground, but when he got closer, he could tell she was trembling. He stopped.

"Hell, Charlotte, please tell me you're not afraid."

"I can't," she whispered.

Her honesty pierced him, sharper than any knife could have done. He shook his head in disbelief.

She was visibly shaking now, so much so that Judd thought she might faint.

"You can't think I would hurt you?"

"I've already told you, I know you will hurt me, Judd Hanna. But not in the way that you mean."

"Then what *are* you afraid of?"

"That someday I'll think of you and won't be able to recall your face."

Her words were like a kick in the gut. Without thinking, he reached for her, thrusting his fingers through her hair and tilting her face to his.

"God help us both, lady. If you intend to run, do it now."

But Charlotte didn't run. On the contrary. She took

a step forward, and then another, until she could feel the warmth of his body against the thrust of her breasts.

"Are you going to make love to me?" she whispered.

"Only if you want me, Charlie."

She sighed. "I must be out of my mind."

"Not yet," Judd said. "But you will be."

He lowered his head.

It was nothing like Charlie had expected. Having based her entire experience on making love with Pete Tucker's gropes and kisses, she wasn't prepared for this man. Somewhere between their first kiss and her next heartbeat, she lost her voice and what was left of her mind. The heat of his mouth pulled at her senses. His hands, moving upon her breasts, then across her shoulders and down her back, lay claim to all that they touched. He moved, pinning her between the wall and his body, then lifted the hem of her gown and cupped her backside with both hands. The hard ridge of him rode between the juncture of her thighs, and as she arched against the pressure, she thought she might die. So long—it had been so long.

In the midst of their passion lay a truth Judd couldn't ignore. He wanted to make love to this woman more than he'd ever wanted anything in his life, but he wasn't prepared to protect her. He clenched his teeth and closed his eyes, willing himself not to explode, yet when she wrapped her legs around him, he buried his face against the curve of her neck and groaned.

"Oh, Charlotte."

Her breath was little more than brief gasps. Her head was tilted back, exposing the slender column of her throat. The knowledge that she was so far gone this fast was almost more than he could bear. But while he wouldn't let himself take that last step with her, there was no way he was going to deny her the ride. He slid his hand between them until he heard her gasp.

Seconds later, she let out a soft moan as she followed the path of his touch, and when, moments later, she collapsed in his arms, he scooped her up and carried her down the hall to her bed.

The aftermath was uncomfortable for both of them. Judd was still aching to the back of his teeth, needing a release he wasn't going to get, and Charlie was stunned by her uninhibited response to a man who'd given her pleasure while taking none of his own. The moment he laid her down on the bed, she covered her face.

"Why?" she whispered. "Why did you let me do that alone?"

Judd moved her hands, forcing her to look at him.

"I wasn't prepared to protect you," he said. "And I damn sure wasn't going to leave you in the same condition Pete Tucker did."

She groaned. What must Judd think of her? She was the one who would have suffered the consequences, yet one touch from this man and her good sense had completely disappeared. She rolled over, then sat up on the side of the bed, smoothing her hair and her gown at the same time, too embarrassed to face him.

Judd sighed.

"Charlotte?"

She stilled, waiting for the rest of his question.

"Look at me...please."

She bit her lip, then looked up.

"For the love of God, don't be sorry that happened."

She shook her head in disbelief.

"How can I?" she asked. "You gave me more than just a physical release. You made me remember something I'd almost forgotten."

"What's that?" he asked.

"That I'm not just Wade's sister, or Rachel's mother. You gave me back my sense of self, Judd Hanna, and for that, I will be forever thankful."

Judd groaned, and then took her hand and pulled it to his lips, kissing the curve of her palm before he pushed himself off of the bed. He was halfway to the door when he stopped and turned.

"There's just one other thing you should know," he said.

She held her breath, almost afraid to listen.

"The next time you experience that sense of self you were talking about, I'm going to be so deep inside you, you won't know where you stop and I start."

It wasn't until he closed the door quietly behind him that Charlie realized she was still holding her breath. With his promise still echoing within the silence of her room, she exhaled on a slow, shaky sob and then lay down and pulled the covers up over her head.

Long after Charlie had gone back to sleep, Judd was still in the shower, standing beneath the pounding of a cold, steady spray. Oddly enough, when he finally made it back to bed, he fell asleep almost instantly, sleeping without dreaming until the sun coming in the window woke him to the day.

* * *

Judd smelled the coffee and stretched, reveling in the luxury of getting up to something other than the strident peal of an alarm. Yet when he rolled over to pick up his watch to check the time, he remembered he didn't have a watch anymore. He'd given it to Davie Dandridge. He made a mental note to stop in at the pharmacy today and pick up another one. It didn't have to be fancy. All he needed was for the darn thing to keep time.

He heard the phone ringing as he was getting dressed. Probably Wade. He'd promised to call. He stomped his feet in his boots and headed for the bathroom to wash his face, tucking his shirt in as he went. A short while later he was reaching for a towel when he realized he was no longer alone.

"Well, now, good morning, little girl. Did you get out of bed by yourself again?"

Rachel nodded sleepily, then draped her blanket over one shoulder and lifted her arms to be held.

Judd reached down, lifting her into his arms and cuddling her close to his chest. Still sleepy, she snuggled, laying her head on his shoulder and shifting until the crown of her head was directly beneath his chin. In spite of the bony jut of his collarbone, that seemed to be her favorite spot to lie.

"You're sure something, you know that?" he said softly, and because no one was looking, he gave himself permission to snuggle her back.

Her tousled curls tickled his nose, and once again, he felt her latch on to his shirt with her fist. He knew if he looked, she would probably be sucking her thumb, too. Sweet baby moments. Who would share these with her when he was gone?

Then he sighed. Wade, of course—and Charlie. Who better to watch her grow up than a doting uncle and a loving mother? He started out of the bathroom with her still in his arms, but the closer he got to the kitchen, the more anxious he became. But what if she needed someone and Wade wasn't around? What if she got away from Charlie again as she had before? Who would rescue her then? By the time he got to the kitchen, his gut was in a knot. Last night, he'd held Charlie in his arms and felt this same damn way—this gut-wrenching panic that they would one day need him and he wouldn't be around.

But before he could sort through his feelings, Charlie saw them and smiled. After that, the knot in his gut took another hitch.

"Good morning," Charlie said. "Did she wake you again?"

"No, she just came to watch me shave."

Charlie's smile slipped a bit. "I used to love to watch my daddy shave," she said, then reached for a cup. "Ready for some coffee?"

"Oh, yeah," he said softly, and then he cupped the back of her head, forcing her to look at him. "About last night…"

"Don't," Charlie said. "Don't apologize. Don't make excuses. Just…just…don't ruin something that was special to me."

He hesitated, then Rachel squirmed and the subject was changed.

"'Mallows?" she asked.

Judd grinned as Charlie shook her head.

"No, baby, we don't eat marshmallows for breakfast," Charlie said. "How about some scrambled eggs and jelly toast?"

Her lower lip slid forward. Just as she was beginning to argue, Judd interrupted her train of thought.

"That sounds good to me," he said. "Can I have some of your scrambled eggs?"

The idea of sharing food with this man was intriguing. They'd shared 'mallows. Sharing eggs should be okay, too.

"Ekks," she said, nodding her okay. "With toas."

Charlie giggled. "Ekks and toas it is," she said. "Judd will put you in your high chair while Mommy fixes your breakfast, okay?"

"Do you care if I take her with me to the barn instead? We need to see if that old mama cat had her kittens yet, don't we, baby girl?"

"Let me take her to the bathroom first, and you've got a deal," Charlie said.

Judd poured himself a cup of coffee while he waited for them to come back. And all the while he was sipping and staring out the window, he kept trying to picture himself in this role for at least the next fifty years. Oddly enough, the thought didn't panic him as it once might have. What would it be like, he wondered, to go to bed and wake up beside this woman for the rest of his life? To laugh with her and cry with her and even grow old with her?

"Here you go," Charlie said. "One busy little girl, ready to start your day."

Judd picked her up and started outside. The moment they got off the porch, he swung her up on his shoulders, letting her straddle his neck.

"Hang on tight, baby girl," he said, and planted both his hands in the center of her back to keep her steady.

Rachel laughed aloud and fisted her hands in his hair to hang on.

"Ouch, ouch, ouch," he yelped. "Don't pull Daddy's hair."

The moment it came out of his mouth, he groaned, thankful that no one had heard the Freudian slip.

The word *daddy* was foreign to Rachel, and the notion of being this high off the ground was too exciting for anything else.

"See da cows?"

Judd sighed. "Yes, honey. I see the cows. Now, if I could only see what was wrong with this mess inside my head, we'd all be a lot better off."

A short while later, they headed back to the house to tell Mommy that the Franklin homestead was four kittens richer than it had been last night.

But when they got inside, Judd learned that Charlie had some news of her own. Once Rachel was eating, Charlie served them, as well.

"Looks great," Judd said. "I feel sorry for Wade, missing out on all of this."

Charlie shrugged. "He's used to my cooking. It's nothing special to him."

"If he had to live on his own, he'd think differently," Judd said. "By the way, didn't I hear the phone ring earlier?"

Charlie was shoving her eggs around on her plate, trying to think of a way to bring up the idea she'd had. His question gave her just the right spot.

"Yes, it was Wade. Said he'd be home to shower and change after nine." Then she pushed her plate aside and leaned forward, ready to state her case before Judd could change the subject. "I had an idea this morning."

Judd started to smile, but the seriousness of her expression changed his mind.

"Oh? About what?" he asked.

"I've overheard you and Wade talking about Raymond. You know, about the fact that maybe someone from his past is responsible for what happened to him."

"That's right, although it is just a theory," Judd said.

"And a good one," Charlie added. "Which brings me to my idea. I wondered how you were going to check that out? Are you going to interview people he grew up with, or just talk to Raymond again?"

"Probably a little of both," Judd said. "Although, to be honest, I doubt we're going to get much more out of Shuler. I get the feeling he's not telling us the whole truth, but he's definitely not ready to talk about it."

"I could help," she said.

Judd looked startled. The idea of putting Charlie in any sort of danger, however remote, wasn't happening.

"Oh, I don't know," he said, and then the disappointment on her face made him add, "What did you have in mind?"

"The library."

"What?"

"The library. There're more than fifty years of newspapers on microfiche, and I think there's a copy of every Call City Cougar since 1907."

"What's a Call City Cougar?" Judd asked, intrigued in spite of himself.

"The school yearbook. I know it's a long shot, but maybe it would be a place to start."

Judd started to smile.

Charlie sighed. "Don't laugh at me," she said.

"No, you misunderstand," Judd said. "It's a damned good idea. In fact, it's better than the one that I had. So how about we do this together?" Then he remembered Rachel. "What about her? I don't think she'll do too well in a place where she's supposed to be quiet."

Charlie was so excited that he'd agreed that she was almost giggling.

"Oh, we have a neighbor a couple of miles down the road. Mrs. Miller? You know the place. She lives in that green-and-white house with the two cedar trees in the front yard. She loves to baby-sit for me. I've already called her…just to make sure she was free."

"Okay, then, Nancy Drew. It's a date."

Charlie looked a little surprised, and then chuckled. Nancy Drew, indeed. Granted, her idea to research the town's written history was hardly on the same level as the renowned fictional sleuth, but it was heady stuff just the same.

Chapter 10

"Wow," Charlie muttered as she and Judd entered the library. "Would you take a look at Wilma!"

Judd looked at the woman behind the check-out counter. "I see her, but what am I supposed to be looking at?"

"That red hair used to be mousy brown with some big streaks of gray. And I don't ever remember seeing her dress like that."

Judd still didn't see anything particularly unusual. "You mean that purple flowered thing?"

"It's so short!" Charlie hissed. "I can almost see her knees."

Judd grinned. "Now, Charlie, you're complaining to the wrong person. I've always been a leg man."

Charlie blushed. "That's not what I meant," she said. "I wasn't criticizing her, I was just surprised, that's all."

At that point, Wilma looked up, then smiled and waved.

"Good morning, Charlotte," she said. "Did you come to pick out some more books for that little sweetheart of yours?"

"No, ma'am," Judd said. "I thought I'd pick them out for myself this time."

It was hard to say who looked more shocked, Charlie or Wilma. And then Judd grinned and Charlie regained enough sense to introduce him.

"Wilma, this incorrigible man is Judd Hanna. He's acting deputy while Hershel is on his honeymoon."

Wilma's eyes suddenly rounded. "Oh! I know who you are," she cried. "You're the man who saved little Rachel from that awful bull."

This time it was Judd's turn to blush. "It's a pleasure to meet you," he said, then quickly changed the subject. "We need to look at everything you might have pertaining to Call City and its citizens over the past twenty…maybe even twenty-five years."

Wilma pivoted sharply, patting her hair as she went, just to make sure it was all still in place, and headed for the microfiche. Her step was light and there was a slight sway to her backside that hadn't been there before. The changes in her appearance were to be expected, of course. After all, she was no longer a virgin. She'd looked upon the naked male form and survived. She was now officially a woman. As for her hairdo, Audie Murphy, the World War II hero-turned-movie-star, had always been her idea of a real man. The change in color was her own personal "red badge of courage" for seeing Raymond Shuler naked.

She flipped on the power to a microfiche screen and then turned.

"Any particular thing you'd be looking for?" she asked.

"Any stories or articles pertaining to Raymond Shuler," Judd said.

She gasped, then put her hand to her bosom, much in the same way she'd done when she'd opened the front door and seen him lying on her steps.

"Oh, my! Does this have to do with his abduction? Is this part of the investigation?"

Judd hesitated. "In a way."

Wilma looked at Charlie, as if she'd suddenly become a stranger, and lowered her voice.

"Is it all right...to talk in front of her, I mean?"

Judd grinned. "Yes, ma'am. In fact, this angle of the investigation was actually Charlie's idea."

"Well, now," Wilma said, eyeing Charlie with renewed respect. "And all this time I thought you were just a sweet little thing with that darling baby." Although they were the only three people in the library, she looked over her shoulder before she spoke. "If there's anything else you need...anything at all...just ask me. I'll stand watch at the front desk. If I see anyone coming, I'll tap three times."

It was all Judd could do not to laugh. "Uh...maybe the better idea would be for you to play it cool, ma'am. You know...go about your business as if we weren't here?"

Wilma's little round eyes widened even more. "Yes! Right! That way word won't get out and the criminal will be caught unaware!"

"That's the way it usually works," Judd said. "So, if you don't mind, we'll get to work."

"Wilma, isn't there a complete set of Cougar yearbooks in the library?" Charlie asked.

Wilma clapped her hands. "Yes! Good idea, Charlotte. Follow me."

"I'll be over there," Charlie said, pointing to a nearby table as Wilma bustled away. Then she realized there was something she hadn't asked. "Uh... Judd?"

"What?"

"Exactly what am I looking for?"

"Start with the years Shuler would have been in high school," he said. "Anytime you find mention of his name, mark it. We'll look at the stuff together, later."

She nodded and started to walk away when he called to her.

"Charlie."

She turned.

"You're the first person I've worked with since Dan was killed."

Her expression froze. "Oh, Judd, I didn't..."

"No, it's not that. In fact, it feels pretty good to have someone like you backing me up."

She smiled, then lifted her chin. "I can't shoot worth a plug nickel, but I'm okay with my fists."

He nodded, remembering the selfless way in which she'd been willing to run down a bull to save her child.

"Yeah, lady, I'll just bet that you are."

They stared at each other in silence—remembering. It was Wilma's stage-voice hiss that broke the spell.

"Charlotte...I have everything ready now."

Charlie blinked, then pointed toward the table where Wilma was waiting. "I suppose I should—"

Judd took a deep breath. "Yeah, and I need to—"

Neither felt the need to finish the sentence they'd started, and by some unspoken word of mutual agreement, they parted company, leaving Judd on his own at the microfiche screens. But as the morning passed, the sound of flipping pages and the occasional sigh from the woman behind him was reminder enough that he wasn't really on his own—not anymore.

It was getting close to noon when Judd looked up. Rubbing his neck, he wearily rolled his head and then stood and strolled over to the table where Charlotte was sitting.

"Find anything?"

She shrugged. "Plenty of pictures, but I don't know if they mean anything. How about you?"

He shook his head. "Nothing that seems to connect," he said, adding, "Shuler's old man was a power in this town, wasn't he?"

Charlie frowned. "I guess. I don't really remember him. I think he died when I was a little girl."

"Well, let's see what you've got," Judd said, and dropped into a chair beside her.

There were the usual group photos.

Raymond at the county fair with his FFA steer.

Raymond as a sophomore on the Cougar baseball team.

Raymond as a junior and starting quarterback of the Cougar football team.

Raymond as a senior and captain of the basketball team.

Judd paid particular attention to the candid photos of the students, looking for a continuing thread, but there didn't seem to be anything other than the fact that Raymond Shuler was a big man on campus.

"He must have been quite a ladies' man," Charlie said.

Judd paused, his interest piqued.

"Why do you say that?" he asked.

"Just look. He's in lots of pictures with lots of girls, but never the same girl twice."

Judd stared, then started to grin. "Like I said, lady. You're really good at this."

Charlie was pleased by the praise. "Does it mean anything?" she asked.

"I don't know," Judd said. "But it's definitely a character trait that he's either overcome or kept hidden."

Her eyes widened. "Oh! I see what you mean!" Then she pointed to one particular picture. "Look, isn't this Wilma?"

Judd pulled the yearbook closer, peering at the small typeface beneath the photo.

"Damned if it's not," he said, then looked up at the librarian, eyeing her with renewed interest. "Hey Wilma, got a minute?" he called.

She spun, instantly pressing her finger to her lips to indicate quiet, then bustled toward him. Judd grinned. Again, the need for quiet seemed moot, since they were the only ones in the room.

"Sorry," he said.

Her lips pursed as she smoothed the fabric of her dress across the front of her belly.

"Did you find anything?" she whispered.

"Nothing obvious," Judd said, and then pointed to the picture in the yearbook Charlie was holding. "Isn't this you?"

She peered over his shoulder, then frowned. "My goodness, I haven't looked at that thing in years. Yes, it's me. I was president of the debate club that year."

"Isn't that Raymond with his arm around you?"

She peered closer, then blushed. "Why yes, I suppose that it is."

Judd watched her closely. She seemed suddenly nervous, when before she'd been so assured.

"Did you two date?"

She began to stammer. "Not really...I mean we never...uh, we barely kissed...and that was only once or twice." Then she regained her composure, reminding herself that she was a grown woman. So she had a past. All women of the world had pasts. "Raymond was a ladies' man," she said loftily. "He passed briefly through my life. It meant nothing."

Charlie stifled a grin and turned her attention to another yearbook, but Judd wasn't through pursuing the issue.

"How about these?" he asked, pointing to the other photos in which Raymond was either hugging or kissing a different girl. "Where are they now?"

Wilma looked a little closer. "Well, let's see. That was Anna Mankin—she's Anna Stewart now. I think she lives in Dallas. And this one, oh...what was her name? Mary Lee, that's right, Mary Lee Howards. She's dead. Died in a car wreck about ten years ago."

Judd made a few notes now and then, but mostly just listened as Wilma regaled them with stories of Raymond Shuler's past. And the longer he sat, the more convinced he became that somewhere within the pages of these books was the answer to what had happened to Raymond. He was just at the point of stopping the stories when she mentioned a name that caught his interest again. Not because he suspected a culprit, but because the woman on the page was so foreign to the one he knew now.

"This is Judy," Wilma said. "You know her."

Judd looked at the tall, elegant girl with dark brown hair and frowned, trying to place that vivacious smile with someone he'd met. She looked vaguely familiar, but the recognition didn't come.

"No, ma'am, I don't think I do," he said.

Charlie clutched his arm. "Sure you do, Judd. That's Judith Dandridge. You know…Davie's aunt."

"You're kidding," he muttered, and pulled the book closer. "She's certainly changed."

Wilma frowned. "I hadn't thought of it, but I suppose you're right. Of course, she's a pharmacist now, and that's almost like a doctor. She has a responsibility to look her professional best. It's a matter of trust, don't you know?"

Judd nodded. "Yes, ma'am. I suppose that's so."

Charlie was still leafing through the pages of Raymond's senior year when she paused.

"Uh, Wilma, wasn't Judith in the same class as you and Raymond?"

Wilma nodded.

"How come she doesn't have a senior picture?"

Wilma frowned. "Why, that can't be. She graduated with us. I remember because she stood in front of me during the processional and I couldn't see over her head. She's very tall, you know."

Wilma turned through several pages, flipping back and forth. Suddenly she stopped.

"Oh, I remember now. Judy and her folks were in some sort of accident, I think. She was bunged up pretty good. I remember she had a lot of scratches and bruises. I think the last two months of our senior year, she was home-schooled.''

"What does that mean?" Judd asked.

Charlie answered. ''For whatever reason, a student is identified as having some sort of handicap that prevents them from attending regular school, so a teacher is assigned and the student does all of his or her lessons at home, with tutorial sessions from the assigned teacher, of course.''

Judd's eyes narrowed thoughtfully. Maybe that was what wiped the smile off of Judith Dandridge's face.

"It must have been a pretty severe accident," he said. "Lucky it didn't cripple her. Were her parents hurt, too?"

Wilma frowned. "No. That was the strange part. Judith was the only one who was injured. Maybe she was in the back seat or something. If I knew at the time, I'm afraid I don't remember now." And then she added, "I do remember that they got a new car afterward."

Judd nodded, accepting the plausibility of the story, but unable to get over the change. It was like looking at two separate women. One with long, flowing hair and a form-fitting dress, the other with greying hair shorn and straight, with no-nonsense clothes. Somewhere along the way, life had wiped the smile right off her face.

He looked at the boy who was in the picture with her. "So, Raymond and Judith dated, too."

Wilma frowned. "Not really. In fact, as I recall, Judy had a boyfriend in another town. I think it used to bug Raymond." Then she added, "Raymond's daddy spoiled him, you know. He had everything he ever wanted." She looked at the picture and amended her statement. "Except Judy, of course."

"Wonder why she never got married?" Charlie asked.

Wilma's frown deepened. "There's nothing wrong with the unmarried state. I had offers, but I stayed single."

"Guess you never found that special someone, huh?" Judd asked, and then glanced at Charlie before turning away.

Charlie's heart skipped a beat. What had that look meant? Was he trying to tell her something about the case—or was it something entirely different? Something that had to do with her and him? She pushed her chair back, then stood.

"I need to stretch my legs."

Judd watched her go, saying nothing about the abruptness of her departure. He looked back at the picture of Raymond, standing beneath a large shady tree with his arms around a young, smiling girl. Poor Judith Dandridge. He could relate. Life had kicked him in the teeth a few times, too. He shoved the book aside and leaned forward, rubbing his eyes with the heels of his hands.

"Do you have a headache?" Wilma asked. "It's probably that microfiche screen. It always gives me a headache."

"Yes, ma'am," Judd said. "It'll go away once my eyes are rested."

"I have some over-the-counter painkillers," Wilma said, and hurried toward the back room, anxious to please. A few moments later, she was back with a plastic cup full of water and an industrial-size bottle of pills. "Here you go," she said. "Help yourself."

A faint but pleasant scent of something citrus wafted past her as she handed him the bottle.

"Nice perfume," he said as he shook some pills out in his hand.

Wilma blushed and patted her hair. "Why, thank you, but I'm not wearing any today."

"Really?" Judd said. "I thought I smelled citrus."

"Oh! That's the liquid hand soap in the bathroom. I washed my hands before I got your medicine. Can't be too careful, you know. Germs live on everything."

Judd nodded. It wasn't until the pills were halfway down his throat that he remembered what Raymond had said about smelling oranges when he'd been tied up. He choked, then took another sip of water.

"Are you all right?" Wilma asked, thumping him firmly on the back.

When Judd could speak without coughing, he nodded. "Just swallowed them the wrong way, I guess."

She smiled, pleased with herself that she'd been standing right there when he'd choked. She couldn't get over what a change her life had taken since she'd seen a naked man. From her hair to her clothes, and now this. He'd been choking a lot. If she hadn't been there to pound his back, there was no telling what might have happened. Today she could go home and write in her journal that she'd saved a man's life.

"So…where did you get that hand soap?" Judd asked.

Wilma frowned. She'd been preparing herself for gratitude, not another question. Then she shrugged. This was another good reason why she'd never married. There was no predicting the intricacies of the male mind.

"I believe I purchased it at one of the pharmacies. It was on sale."

Great, Judd thought. That meant almost anyone could have some.

He nodded. "It's nice."

Then Judd noticed Charlie going out the front door. From the way she was moving, something had obviously caught her attention. He stood, curious as to what it might be.

"I see Charlie's about ready to leave, and I think we've exhausted the possibilities here. Thanks for your help, Wilma."

She nodded importantly. "I'll keep it under my hat," she said, and then grinned and patted her hair. "Figuratively speaking, of course."

Judd grinned back, then followed Charlie out the door. By the time he got outside, she was on her knees in the grass, playing with a small brown puppy.

"Who's your friend?" he asked.

Charlie glanced at him, and then the puppy suddenly barked and she refocused her attention to the dog.

"Isn't she the cutest thing you ever saw?"

Judd squatted down beside her, playfully scratching the small puppy's ears while looking at Charlie's face.

"Yes, she sure is," he said softly.

It took a moment for the compliment to sink in, and then when it did, she blushed, hesitating for the right thing to say.

"Judd, can I ask you something?" she finally asked.

"Sure."

"Are you just playing with my feelings?"

He hadn't expected to be put on the spot so succinctly, but since he'd known Charlotte Franklin, he'd come to expect nothing less than total honesty from her. He rocked back on his heels.

"Hell, Charlotte, I would have thought what happened between us last night was a little more than playing."

Her blush heightened. Remembering the wantonness of her behavior was hard to face, but she wasn't sorry that it had happened.

Someone yelled at the puppy from across the street. They watched as it ran back to its yard, then Charlie stood and brushed off the knees of her pants.

"Are we through?" she asked.

He was a little taken aback that she'd dropped the subject so quickly.

"Yeah, we're through," he said.

She lifted her head, shading her eyes from the afternoon sun as she swept a stray lock of hair away from her face.

"That's what I thought," she said, and got into his Jeep without another word.

It took him a moment to realize that there was another connotation that could have been put on her question and his answer, and when he did, it angered him. As far as he was concerned, the "we" in their relationship had yet to happen, so there wasn't any damned way that "they" could be through.

He got into his Jeep and slammed the door shut with a bang.

"Thank you for your help in there today."

She nodded.

He wanted that earlier camaraderie back, but it was nowhere in sight. Silently cursing himself and the world in general, he reached down and started the engine, then put it in gear.

"Is there anything else you need to do before I take you home?"

"I'd like to stop by the pharmacy. I need to buy a couple of birthday cards."

He backed into the street, then shifted gears and took off, leaving a strip of black rubber on the pavement behind him.

Charlie wisely kept silent all the way to the store.

After spending the morning researching Raymond Shuler's history, it was a little disconcerting to see him getting out of his car. His wife, Betty, was behind the wheel, obviously chauffeuring him around. The look on his face was just shy of furious, and Charlie wondered what had happened to set him off.

"There's Raymond," Charlie said. "But he doesn't look very happy."

Judd looked up. Sure enough, the man was getting out of his car and then hobbling up the curb and onto the street.

"You're right, he doesn't," Judd said. He'd seen that look on men's faces before, and it had usually ended in a shouting match or a fistfight. "I think I'll go inside with you, just in case."

Charlie frowned. "Just in case of what?"

But Judd was already getting out of the vehicle. She had no other option but to follow.

They could hear Raymond shouting before they opened the door, and not even the jingle of the entry bell was enough to slow him down.

"I'm telling you for the last time, you keep that retard away from my house. I'm sick and tired of having my view spoiled by the sight of him digging through my garbage like some damned animal.''

Judith's face was completely devoid of color, and although she had yet to speak, he could tell she was livid. The veins in her neck were protruding, and her fingers were curled into fists. When she made a move toward a display of crutches and canes, Judd bolted.

''What's going on here?'' he asked, aiming his question at Shuler.

''Nothing that concerns you,'' Raymond said.

''That's where you're wrong, Mr. Shuler. I could hear shouting all the way out on the street, which definitely constitutes disturbing the peace. And when I came in, I witnessed you verbally abusing Miss Dandridge. There's a place and time for everything, Shuler, and this is definitely not it.''

Shuler's face flushed a dark angry red as he pointed a finger in Judith's face.

''That boy she keeps is trespassing on my property. He goes through the garbage cans on the block like some animal. I warned her before that if it didn't stop, I was going to have him committed.''

Judith took a deep breath, and Judd could tell it was all she could do to remain civil.

''He was only looking for cans,'' she said. ''And he wasn't stealing. Betty said it was all right for him to take them.''

Raymond waved his cane in the air, unaware of any agreement and unwilling to admit he was wrong.

''I don't know anything about an agreement between you and my wife, but I'm telling you now, for the very last time, if you don't keep him off my property, you'll be sorry.''

Judd grabbed the cane out of Shuler's hand.

"Give me that," he said shortly. "Now, you listen to me, or you're likely to be the one who winds up sorry. It sounds to me like you need to get your facts straight before you make accusations. If your wife gave Davie permission to recycle your aluminum cans, then it seems to me he was within his rights to be on your property. It doesn't take a lot of guts to threaten a woman, but you're welcome to try that on me."

Raymond blinked, taken aback by the suggestion.

"Don't be ridiculous," he muttered. "I have no quarrel with you."

"You don't have one with her, either," Judd said, pointing to Judith. "Now, I suggest you apologize to Miss Dandridge, then you take yourself home."

Shuler was so angry he was shaking. He didn't like to be thwarted, and he didn't like to be told what to do, but Judd Hanna had done just that, and without raising his voice. He glared at Judith, then turned to Judd.

"My cane," he said, holding out his hand.

Judd handed it back to him, then stepped aside, watching as the man stomped out the door.

The moment he was gone, Charlie rushed to Judith's side.

"Judith, are you all right? Is there anything we can do?"

But Judith didn't answer. Instead, she stood without moving, watching until Shuler was out of her store. Just as he was getting into his car, her pager went off. She unclipped it from her pocket and read the display, then looked up.

"Is there something I can help you with?" Judith asked.

Charlie realized Judith was not going to acknowledge her offer.

"No, I think I can find what I need on my own," she said.

"Take your time," Judith said. "I have to return this call, then I must go look for Davie. He's probably frightened."

"I'll go," Judd said.

Judith looked startled. She glanced at her pager again and knew the call was probably important. Her duties as a pharmacist were warring with her duties to Davie. Finally, she relented.

"I would appreciate it," she said, and hurried away.

As soon as she was gone, Charlie turned.

"Now do you see what I mean? Poor Judith—and poor Davie. I'll bet Raymond scared him to death."

Judd frowned. "When you get through here, do you mind walking down to the P.D.?"

"Of course not."

"I'm going to let Wade know what happened, then see if I can find Davie. I'll take you home later."

"If I'm not in the office, I'll be across the street at the café. It's almost noon and I'm starving."

Judd looked startled and glanced at his watch, only to realize he still didn't have one. That was something else he would do, but later, when he had more time.

"Sorry," he said. "I didn't mean to forget to feed you."

She shrugged. "I can take care of myself. I've been doing it now for years."

Judd left, wishing they hadn't parted on such stilted

terms. He sighed as he slid behind the steering wheel and started the engine. As always, it seemed that when he was needed most, he was always running away.

Chapter 11

Judith came from the back of the pharmacy. When she realized Charlie was still there, she looked uncomfortable, as if she didn't know whether to remark on what had just happened or not. But when Charlie calmly inquired about a particular item, she began to relax.

"Are these all the men's watches you have?" Charlie asked, pointing toward a small display on a rotating stand.

"No, there are some in this case over here," Judith said, and pulled a key from her pocket as she moved across the room.

Charlie followed, leaning against the counter and peering down through the glassed-in top, then smiling to herself as she saw the merchandise there.

"That one," she said. "The one in the upper right-hand corner. May I see it, please?"

Judith took it out and laid it on the counter, watching curiously as the grin on Charlie's face continued to widen.

"How much?" Charlie asked.

Judith upended the box to look. "It's on sale—$39.95."

Charlie did a little mental math, calculating what she could cut on the grocery items, and knew she could swing it.

"I'll take it," she said.

Judith didn't comment on her choice, and Charlie didn't bother to explain.

"Wrap it up, will you?" Charlie asked.

"Certainly," Judith said, and then hesitated as she reached for the wrapping paper. "Is it a birthday gift?"

"No. Just a replacement for something lost."

At that moment, Judith realized who this was for.

"I'm sorry," she said stiffly. "I didn't realize. I can give you a bigger discount."

"No," Charlie said. "It was already on sale. Besides, in this case, I think the man is well worth the money."

For a moment, the two women stared at each other, then as if by some unspoken sign, they looked away. Charlie sorted through the birthday cards she'd come to buy while Judith wrapped the watch. A few minutes later, Charlie paid for her purchases and left. Somewhere down the street, there was a cheeseburger and fries with her name on it and a man who'd stolen her heart.

Call City wasn't all that large, but there were a lot of alleys and shortcuts that Judd wasn't familiar with. He figured his best bet was to start at Shuler's house and work his way back downtown toward the pharmacy, where he suspected Davie would eventually end up.

When he began his search, he was confident that, before long, he would see Davie. But when ten, and then fifteen minutes had passed with no sign of him, he began to worry. He tried to put himself in Davie's shoes, but couldn't summon the image. Davie would always be an innocent, and even at six, Judd had been worldly and hardened far beyond his years.

He rolled down the windows and slowed his vehicle to a crawl, listening intently for the sound of a squeaky wheel or the rattle of cans. But he soon realized that he would not be able to hear anything over the sound of his engine. It would take longer to search on foot, but he didn't see any other options.

He parked at a curb in front of the veterinary clinic, then killed the engine and got out. He stood for a couple of minutes, eyeing the lay of the area and trying to see it through the eyes of a child.

Where would I go...if I was sad...and I was scared...and I was six?

He started walking, moving in and out of the patches of shade dappled along the sidewalk. Up ahead, a woman was on her knees, digging in a flower bed. Judd paused.

"Ma'am, have you seen Davie Dandridge?"

She leaned back and pushed her hat off her forehead.

"Who?" she asked.

"Davie Dandridge...the man who collects the aluminum cans?"

"Oh, you mean that simple boy? No, not today."

Judd tipped his hat and hid a frown as he continued

up the street. *Simple.* The word had rolled off the woman's tongue without thought, rather callously describing someone who didn't quite fit in this world. But as Judd walked, he realized it could be a good word, after all. There wasn't really anything wrong with Davie. He wasn't so different; his life was just simpler. He wondered if Davie's mother had known there was something wrong with her baby—if that's the reason she gave him away. Then he shrugged off the thought. There was no reason to feel sorry for Davie when he didn't feel sorry for himself.

He kept moving, stopping now and then to question people in their yards, and some who were walking down the streets. It wasn't until he neared the junkyard at the south edge of town that he saw a narrow set of tracks on the shoulder of the road. Tracks from a little red wagon. Davie couldn't be far.

He walked until he came to the six-foot board fence surrounding the yard, then followed the wagon tracks east. A short distance away, he could see a large gap in the fence where several boards had been removed. He stopped and looked in. There, in the distance, he caught a glimpse of something red. He took off his Stetson, then slipped through the fence. When he was on the other side, he settled it firmly back on his head and stood, examining the lay of the land.

It wasn't a particularly safe place for a child to be, even if the child was over six feet tall. The rusting hulks of car bodies were stacked two, sometimes three high, and in other places, salvage had yet to be stripped down. He moved through the narrow alleyway, keeping his eye on the little red wagon and listening for the sound of voices. It wasn't until he got a bit closer that he realized he could hear someone crying. He frowned. Damn Raymond Shuler's sorry hide. He *had* scared the kid—scared him half to death.

And then Judd saw him, sitting behind the wheel of a '57 Chevy, hunched over a broken steering wheel and staring intently through the opening where the windshield had been. He took a deep breath and started toward him.

"Hey, mister, could you give me a ride?"

The sound of Judd's voice startled Davie. In the middle of a sob, he suddenly jumped, his eyes wide and tear-filled, his mouth slack with fright. He recognized the man. It was the man who'd given him his clock. And then he looked closer. The man was making a fist with his hand and was holding up his thumb. Davie suddenly smiled. He knew what that meant.

"Yes. I can give you a ride," Davie said. "Get into my car and I will drive you away."

Ignoring the layers of dirt and rust, Judd stepped across a thick patch of weeds and crawled into the passenger side of the seat.

"Nice day for a drive, isn't it?" Judd said.

Davie nodded. "I'm running away," he said, and shifted pretend gears—the gearshift had long disappeared.

"Why?" Judd asked. "Won't your aunt Judy be sad?"

Davie's faint smile crumpled. "I love Aunt Judy," he mumbled, and then lay his head on the steering wheel and sobbed.

Judd scooted across the seat and put his arms around Davie's shoulders.

"Then why are you running away from her?" Judd asked.

"Not running away from her," Davie said, sobbing. "That man scared me. I tried to tell him it was okay, but he wouldn't listen."

At that moment, if Raymond Shuler had been anywhere in sight, Judd would have decked him. Damn him for what he'd done to this boy.

"Well, your aunt Judy and I had a long talk with Mr. Shuler," Judd said. "He's sorry he yelled, and he won't be scaring you anymore."

Davie's sobs stopped as suddenly as they'd begun. "He's not mad at me?"

Judd ruffled Davie's hair and smiled. "No, son, he's not going to be mad at you, I promise." Then he took a handkerchief out of his hip pocket and handed it to Davie. "Here, wipe your eyes and blow your nose and I'll walk you back to the pharmacy."

Davie did as he was told, then crawled out of the car and held out his hand as he'd been taught, waiting to be led to safety.

Judd grinned, but there was a lump in his throat as they began walking out of the junkyard. No wonder Judith Dandridge was so protective of this boy. He was far too trusting for the ugliness of this world.

Charlie had just taken her last drink of iced tea when she happened to look out the window of the café and breathed a quick sigh of relief. It was Judd and Davie, walking hand in hand down the sidewalk. She tossed some money on the table and grabbed her things, heading for the door. Outside, she could hear the faint squeak of that wheel and the rattle of cans as Davie pulled his little wagon behind him. She started toward them across the street.

Suddenly, Judith burst out of the pharmacy.

"Davie! Oh, Davie, I was so worried about you," she cried, and pulled him into her embrace. "Where have you been? You know if you get scared, you're supposed to come to me."

But Davie was beyond explanations. He was too happy to be where he belonged.

Charlie bolted up on the sidewalk, her voice light with relief.

"Judd! Where did you find him?"

"Yes, where was he?" Judith asked.

Judd hesitated, knowing that he was probably going to give away one of Davie's secret places, but it was for the kid's own good.

"At the junkyard. He'd commandeered a '57 Chevy. In its day, I imagine it was a real hot ride. In spite of a few missing parts and no wheels, I think he thought he was getting the hell out of Dodge."

Judith groaned. "Davie, darling, you know you aren't supposed to be in that place. You could get hurt."

A corner of Judd's mouth turned up in a smile. "Yeah, and you're going to have to talk to him about picking up hitchhikers, too. However, you don't need to worry about his driving. He keeps his eyes on the road when he's behind the wheel."

Davie lifted his head and smiled at Judd.

"I gave him a ride, Aunt Judy, and then he brought me home."

Charlie inhaled sharply, then looked at Judd, as if seeing him for the very first time. Tears shattered her view of the world. She knew he was tough, and she knew he was strong, and she'd seen him burst into laughter quite often, especially at something Rachel had done. But imagining him in a rusted-out hulk of a car, letting Davie take them on a wild pretend ride? She'd had no idea, until this very moment, how truly gentle this big man must be.

"Well, now," Judith said softly. "That's fine, just fine, Mr. Hanna, and I thank you…more than you will ever know."

Judd smiled and ran his hand over Davie's head, smoothing down that thick shock of flyaway hair.

"It's just part of the job, ma'am," he said, and then looked at Davie. "Besides, he's a pretty interesting kid when you get to know him."

Judith suddenly clenched her jaw. She nodded briefly.

"Yes, he is," she said. "It's just a shame that everyone can't see that. Davie's life would be so much easier." Then she took Davie by the hand. "Come along, Davie. We'll have our lunch now. Tell the deputy thank you for bringing you home."

"Thank you," Davie parroted.

"You're welcome," Judd said. "But remember what we talked about. No more running away, okay?"

Davie nodded, more concerned with food than with remembering promises.

Judd stood on the street, watching as the pair disappeared into the pharmacy. Now that the little drama was over, he felt out of sync and oddly bereft.

"Judd?"

He turned, nervously eyeing the tears in Charlie's eyes, but when she slid her hand into his, the world settled.

"I thought you were ticked off at me."

She arched an eyebrow. "I still may be. I haven't decided. But that doesn't keep me from being proud of you, too."

"Why?"

"You gave Davie something today that I doubt he's ever known before," she said.

"What?"

"Dignity. When you've had it and then lost it, it's a precious thing to get back."

Suddenly, Judd suspected that they were no longer talking about Davie, but about her, instead. He pictured her pregnant and unmarried, having to face down people who knew she'd been dumped. Before he thought, he opened his arms and pulled her close to his chest. Moments later, his voice was shaking as he let her go.

"You're a dangerous woman, Charlotte."

Still reeling from the embrace and unwilling to let him see how much he affected her, she steadied herself by suddenly clutching her purse to her chest.

"I'm think you've been out in the Wyoming sun a little too long," she said. "Dangerous is the last thing I'll ever be."

But Judd shook his head. "That's where you're wrong. A woman can cry *because* of a man—because of what he did or didn't do to her, as the case may be—but when she sheds tears *for* him, it's a dangerous thing."

"Dangerous to whom?" Charlie asked.

"To the man, darlin', to the man. It's then he knows she's seen his weaknesses. After that, there's no defense."

"Have I seen your weaknesses, Judd Hanna?"

His expression darkened. "You've seen enough," he muttered.

"I doubt that," she said, then grabbed his hand. "Now it's time for you, and you're coming with me."

"Where are we going?"

"To get you some food."

The moment she said it, he realized how hungry he was.

"Okay," he said. "But afterward, I need to have someone take me to my Jeep."

Charlie looked around, only then realizing it was gone.

"That's right," she said. "You and Davie walked here. Where is it? Why didn't you drive?"

"It's somewhere on Henson Street, and we walked, because Davie wanted to hold my hand."

The words hit Charlie's heart, just like the sight of her baby's smile. It was all she could do to speak.

"You know what, Judd Hanna? So do I." She held out her hand. "Are you game?"

Judd stood, stunned by the thunder of his own emotions. It was a moment before he could move.

"Hell, yes," he said softly, then his fingers closed around hers with a jerk, as if he were afraid that she'd suddenly disappear.

Charlie exhaled. She didn't know how long this man would stay in their lives, but she'd made up her mind to take whatever he would give and be happy for the gesture.

Wade was sitting at the kitchen table, downing the last of a sandwich, when they walked into the house. Charlie took Rachel to her room to play, while Judd went to the sink to wash his hands.

"How did the day go?" Wade asked. "Did you find Davie okay?"

"Yes, I found him, but I'm not having as much luck with the Shuler case."

Wade shrugged. "For two cents, I'd chuck the whole investigation, but the cop in me knows I can't do it. Besides, I'm sort of curious as to who hated him enough to put that sore on his ass."

Judd nodded. "The man's a real piece of work, all right. He scared that kid so bad, he was trying to run away."

Wade frowned. "Damn." He stood, then gathered his dirty dishes and carried them to the sink. "You know, I always felt a little sorry for Raymond and Betty that they never had any kids, but now I'm thinking it was probably a good thing. He doesn't have a compassionate bone in his body. On another note, I'll be staying in town at night…at least for the next few days until everything settles down."

"After Raymond came back, I thought everything was settled," Charlie said. "Why do you have to stay in town?"

The men turned, unaware that she'd entered the room.

"In hopes of staving off a damned panic," Wade said.

"What kind of panic?" Judd asked.

Wade started to grin. "Well, it started with Harold Schultz's wife. You remember Harold? He's your mechanic, and the guy I brought in drunk the other day."

Judd nodded.

"Anyway, old Harold went missing again today. I tried to tell his wife that he was probably somewhere sleeping off a drunk, but she'd convinced herself that he'd been snatched, just like Raymond. Then, before the hour had passed, some woman had called the department and reported seeing a UFO. One thing led to another, and before I knew it, Mrs. Schultz had theorized that aliens were responsible for Shuler's kidnapping and subsequent return, and that they'd now taken her Harold. From that, hysteria boiled.'' He glanced at his watch. ''And, if I had to guess, I'd say that right about now, all the members of the Call City Southern Baptist Church are together at the church, praying in earnest for Harold's safe return.''

''Lord have mercy,'' Charlie muttered.

Judd laughed aloud. ''You're kidding, right?''

Wade shook his head. ''No, I'm not.''

''But Wade, if the alien theory is to hold any water, exactly what does Harold's wife think the brand is about?'' Charlie asked.

Wade chuckled. ''Funny you should ask. The story highest on the list at the moment is that it stands for the planet they're from. I tried to tell her that living beings from other planets most likely didn't use our alphabet, so putting an *R* on Shuler's butt made no sense. However, by that time, Mrs. Schultz wasn't making any sense, either, so it stood to reason no one would listen to me.''

''Are you sure you don't want me to spell you off tonight? After all, you stayed in town last night,'' Judd said.

''Thanks, but I think a familiar face is best. Hell, if you stepped into this controversy right now, they'd probably find a way to accuse you of being the alien.''

''You're probably right,'' Judd said. ''And in a way, they'd be right. I am a stranger.''

"Not anymore," Charlie said quietly.

"That's right," Wade said. "As far as I'm concerned, you could call up that captain of yours back home and tell him you quit, that you're taking a job in Wyoming."

Judd wondered if he looked as startled as he felt. All the while he'd been staying here, he'd been focusing on the day he would leave. A little unsure of his feelings, he tried to laugh off the comment.

"Yeah, right."

"You laugh," Wade said. "But I'm serious."

Judd turned away, reaching into the cabinet for a glass and filling it with water from the faucet.

"It's something to think about," he said, then took a long drink, purposefully ignoring the startled glance Charlie gave him.

"Well, I'm off," Wade said. "If I go missing, you'll know where to look for me." He pointed up to the sky, then exited the house, still chuckling beneath his breath.

The silence he left behind him was stark and uncomfortable. Charlie began digging through the refrigerator, leaving Judd on his own.

"Need any help?" he finally asked.

"No, I'm fine."

He shoved his hands in his pockets. "If you don't mind, I guess I'll go see what Rachel is up to. I missed seeing that little face today."

Charlie stood, staring down into the sink at the potatoes she was going to peel, and then took a deep breath. *Stay calm. Don't get your hopes pinned on anything resembling a man. That way you won't get yourself hurt.*

It wasn't long before she heard the sound of his

laughter and her baby's giggles coming from the back of the house. She picked up another potato, peeling furiously. Damn the man. He was so under her skin, and she was so going to be hurt.

Charlie came out of the bathroom, fresh from her shower, and peeked in on Rachel. The little girl was sound asleep on her tummy with her rump in the air. As usual, she'd wrapped her blanket around her neck and Charlie slipped inside long enough to pull another one up over her feet.

"Good night, baby girl," she said softly, and blew a kiss into the air before closing the door behind her.

Up the hall, she could hear the faint sounds of a television program in progress, and every now and then, the rattle of a newspaper. She smiled to herself. Just like a man. Trying to do two things at once. Then she amended the thought. If there was anyone who could pull that stunt off, Judd Hanna just might be it.

She smoothed her hands over her hair, then tugged at the hem of her knit pajamas. She started to go back for a robe and then stopped. If she did, she would be too warm, and the pajamas were decent, covering everything that a T-shirt and jeans would cover. She didn't take into consideration the softness of the fabric and the way it clung to her body, or the just-washed soap-and-powder scent she brought with her as she entered the room. She picked up a basket of mending on her way toward her chair, then absently turned on the lamp as she sat.

Judd looked up from his reading, taking careful note of her fresh-scrubbed appearance, as well as the tender curve of her neck as she bent to her task. All evening, he'd been tense, even a little uneasy, wondering how this "family" evening was going to play out. Just he and she—and a baby—it was almost too perfect.

Yet as he sat, looking at her there in the lamplight, a yearning came upon him so strong that it made his heart hurt. Just for a moment, he let himself pretend that this was his life—that Charlotte was his woman, and the baby, their child. It was the pain that came afterward that stunned him. Pain that came from knowing it was only a dream.

He sighed, then made himself return to his reading. Only the words no longer made sense. He couldn't think past the woman on the other side of the room.

Charlie knew he was watching her. She could feel the heat of his gaze, but she was afraid to look up. Too much had been going on between them today to ignore, but she wasn't sure if she was ready to be the instigator. Finally, she gained a sense of control and laid her mending down in her lap. If nothing else, she just needed to hear the sound of his voice.

"Judd?"

He looked up so suddenly, she could tell he hadn't been reading after all.

"What?"

"What makes some people so mean?"

Her question struck a nerve and he flinched. While he suspected she was thinking of Raymond Shuler, his mind automatically went to his own past, and to the man who'd been his father. It was all he could do to answer.

"I don't know."

"Do you think that people are born that way, or do you think it's a thing that they learn?"

Judd sighed. She wasn't going to give up until she got an answer that satisfied her.

"Maybe a little of both," he finally said. "What do you think?"

Her forehead furrowed, and then she dumped her sewing in the basket on the floor and folded her legs up beneath her.

"I think that life does it to them."

He frowned. "What do you mean?"

"Well, I don't think that babies are born with anger and viciousness, do you? I mean—think about it. At first, they're all brand-new—little angels straight from God. It's what happens to them after they get here that cripples their minds and scorches their wings."

Tears suddenly blurred Judd's vision of her face, and he had to focus on something else to keep from crying. The image she'd painted was too real to bear. If he'd ever had wings, they'd been burned off long ago in the fires of his father's hell.

"I guess you're right," he said, and made a fuss with straightening the paper he'd been reading.

"Look at Raymond. According to Wilma, he was born with the proverbial silver spoon in his mouth, and yet it hasn't made him happy. So, you have to ask yourself why. Maybe the things he was taught were self-destructive. Maybe that's why he has this constant need to be the one in control. But the way he treats Davie...I just don't understand it. There's no way a person like Davie could pose any threat."

Judd tossed the paper aside, pinning her with a hard, even stare.

"In spite of the disappointments life has handed you, Charlotte, you have still lived a very sheltered life."

She flushed. "That sounded like an accusation," she muttered.

Judd stood abruptly. "You know, you're right," he said. "You didn't deserve that, and I'm sorry."

Angry with himself, he started to leave when she called out his name.

"Please, Judd...don't go."

He sighed, then stuffed his hands in his pockets and turned to face her.

"Why? You don't deserve to suffer the effects of my moods."

Charlie stood, too, then took his hand, tugging until he returned to his seat.

"Okay," he said wryly. "I'm here. Now what?"

"Talk to me...tell me about you."

He gritted his teeth. On a good day, talking about himself wasn't a thing that he did easily, and tonight, he knew it was the last thing he needed to do. But the look on her face and the plea in her voice kept him seated. He didn't have it in him to deny her a damned thing.

"What do you want to know?"

"For starters, how old are you? Where were you raised? Why have you never married?"

"Thirty-three. Boyington, Kentucky. Didn't find the right woman."

Charlie folded her hands in her lap like a perfect child.

"Well, now," she said. "That was painless, wasn't it?"

He laughed, but something told him she was just getting started.

Chapter 12

"Have you ever been engaged?" Charlie asked.

"No."

She leaned back, eyeing the clean, muscular lines of his body. Then her gaze shifted to his face. Closed expression, dark eyes, strong chin. But, oh so intriguing. Finally she arched an eyebrow and shook her head.

"Are all the women in Tulsa blind, or are they just plain fools?"

"Talk like that could get you in trouble," he said softly, hiding a grin.

Charlie knew she was playing with fire, but she was cold from the inside out and it had been such a long time since she'd been warm.

"What do you do for fun?" she asked.

He frowned. Truthful answers were going to be too revealing, yet he didn't have it in him to lie to her. He sighed. Better tell her the truth and turn her off now than wait until they wound up hurting each other somewhere down the line.

"Not much," he said.

Charlie hesitated. "What do you mean, not much? Do you mean you don't have much time for your hobbies, or are you telling me that you don't indulge at all?"

"Damn it, Charlotte, why does it matter?" he growled.

"Because I never slept with a man I didn't know, and I don't intend to start now."

He froze. *Have mercy. How does a man get past a woman like this?*

Charlie pretended she wasn't flustered by his silence, but the truth was, she was at the borderline of panic. *Oh, God, don't let me lose my nerve now.*

"So, what you're telling me is you do not allow yourself pleasure?" she said.

He couldn't quit staring. Damn the woman, but she was picking him apart at the seams.

"Doesn't look like I need to tell you anything," he muttered. "You're doing a hell of a job on my psyche all by yourself."

Her composure fell. Now she'd done it! She'd made him mad. But the woman inside her wouldn't let up. She stood abruptly, motioning for him to follow.

He eyed it nervously. "What?"

"Come with me."

Muttering under his breath as to the wisdom of letting her call all the shots, he stood.

"Where are we going?"

"Out to play," Charlie said. "It's good for the soul."

* * *

Sweat was running from Charlie's hairline and down the back of her neck. Her pajama top was stuck to her body and there was a big dirty handprint on her shoulder where Judd had tried to push past her on his way to the basket.

"Had enough?" she asked, bouncing the basketball up and down at her feet.

Judd was bent at the waist and clutching his knees, struggling for every breath that he took. His legs felt like jelly and sweat kept running into his eyes, burning and blurring his vision. Charlie, on the other hand, wasn't even breathing hard, and there was a glint in her eyes that warned him she wouldn't give in until he gave up. Finally, he groaned and sat the rest of the way down.

"Was this supposed to be fun?" he muttered.

She grinned. At least now she had his attention. She tossed the ball into the shrubs by the back door and then ambled over to where he was sitting and plopped down beside him.

A cloud of bugs had gathered beneath the halo of light by which they'd been playing. Every now and then, one would make a mistake and fly into the heat, and Judd knew just how they felt. For the first time in his life, he'd taken on more than he could handle. Who the hell could have known it would come in such a deceptive package?

"Are you all right?" Charlie asked.

Judd groaned. "I'll let you know tomorrow."

"I suppose this means you're too tired to mess around?"

He looked up, caught the gleam in her eye, and then laughed. The sound surprised him. He didn't think he'd had that much oxygen left in his brain, but the moment he heard it, he realized how good he felt. Not in his body, but in his heart.

Impulsively, he grabbed her by the shoulders and wrestled her to the ground.

"There isn't a man walking who will admit to that," he said, and pinned her beneath him.

"Eeww," she said. "You stink."

He grinned. "You don't smell so good yourself, sweet cakes. And those pajamas are done for."

She grimaced. "This means another bath. I beat you, so I get to go first."

His grin widened as he rolled off of her and dragged himself to his feet.

"You sure you want the first shower?" he asked.

She frowned. There was a gleam in his eye she didn't like.

"I guess."

He turned and walked toward the side of the house.

"You're sure?" he repeated.

"Yes, for God's sake, I'm sure I want the first bath," she yelled.

She rolled over, intending to get up, but only got as far as her hands and knees before the first blast of water struck.

"Judd! Stop! It's cold! It's cold!"

She darted toward the shadows, but he was right behind, aiming the garden hose straight at her back.

"Because of you, I've been taking cold showers ever since the first night I spent in this house. They won't kill you. Trust me," he yelled.

Charlie was caught. She ran from her car to behind the tree. Once she tried to make a run for the house and got a dose squarely in the face. The chill of the water was no longer an issue. It was justice she wanted now—and she knew just how to get it.

In the middle of a blast, she stopped. Ignoring the shattering cold to her back, she slowly turned, facing Judd without flinching. She watched the grin freeze on his face as she pulled one arm out of her pajama top, and then the other, performing a slow striptease beneath the basketball goal. When she pulled the wet garment over her head and tossed it on top of a nearby bush, the grin on his face slid out of sight.

Her nipples peaked in the chill night air, taunting him from a distance. He groaned and dropped the hose. Water began pooling at his feet, then running toward the bottom of the driveway.

Charlie hooked her thumbs in the waistband of her pajama bottoms and started toward him, letting the natural sway of her hips entice him even further.

When she was close enough to feel his breath on her cheek, she lifted her face, offering him whatever he wanted. She saw him shudder, and when he blinked, she made her move. Seconds later, the water hose was in her hand. Before Judd could move, she had him dead to rights.

Water went up his nose, in his eyes and down the middle of his belly. He coughed, then laughed, and then choked again when the water went down his throat.

"You will be sorry," he croaked, and darted off to the side.

But her aim was as good as his had been. Before long, Judd was soaked to the skin. Finally, he held up his hands in defeat.

"You win, darlin', in every way known possible to

man. I secede. I give. I'm crying uncle and wolf…even Tom, Dick and Harry.''

Charlie grinned. ''Those last three don't match the others.''

''What do I have to do?'' he begged.

She turned off the water, then turned. ''Talk to me,'' she said softly. ''Tell me why you don't ever play.''

He stilled. Didn't she ever give up? Then he knew by the look on her face that she would stand there all night until he answered.

''Because the noise would have made Joe Hanna mad. And when he got mad, he took it all out on me.''

Charlie didn't have to ask who Joe Hanna was. The look he wore now was the same expression he'd had that day in the kitchen when he'd admitted his father had beaten him every day of his life.

''Oh, Judd, I am so sorry.''

''It wasn't your fault.''

''That's right, it wasn't,'' she said softly. ''So the next time I offer you friendship, don't be afraid to accept. I'm not going to hit you or curse you. In fact, I've been trying to love you for several days now, but you're making it very difficult. I'll admit, I'm scared half to death of being hurt again myself, but there's something I know that you don't.''

''What's that?''

''People can and will hurt you. It's happened to me. That's the ugly part of life. But there are also those who will love you—so much so that you can't even imagine the joy. However, if you're afraid to trust again, if you quit on yourself, then whoever hurt you ultimately wins, even if they're no longer in your life.''

Judd stood, stunned by what she'd just said. And in that moment, he felt purged of a horrible weight.

"How did you get to be so smart?" he growled.

"I'm not smart. Just a woman who knows how to love."

His heart skipped a beat. He could hear the words coming up his throat before they ever came out of his mouth, yet once uttered, he knew he'd never be the same.

"Charlotte."

She took a step toward him. "Yes?"

"If I ask you a question, will you tell me the truth?"

She blinked, a little startled by the way he'd turned the tables on her. Then she nodded.

"Yes, I will do that."

"If I asked, would you make love with me?"

She took a deep breath and then lifted her chin.

"If you asked, I might."

He started to smile.

"Charlotte?"

"What?"

"Will you make love with me?"

She held out her hand.

Somewhere between the back door and his bedroom, they came out of what was left of their clothes. The soft, even sounds of the baby's breathing were evident as Judd picked Charlie up and carried her across the threshold into his room. He laid her on the bed and then turned and locked the door. The message was clear.

"Now it's just you and me, babe," Judd whispered.

Charlie reached for him, pulling him down until they were lying side by side, looking intently into each other's face. Strands of her wet hair still clung to her cheek and he brushed them away, then ran his hand along the curve of her cheek, then the length of her neck, and finally, the thrust of her breast.

She arched toward him, offering herself in every way.

He grunted briefly, as if he'd gotten a sucker punch to the gut, and then gave himself up to the dance. He stole the first kiss, she gave up the second. After that, there was no keeping track. Time ceased, becoming nothing but a bridge to the next caress. Whispers passed between them in the dark, taking pleasure to a new and dangerous level. Judd was moving into a place where thought ceased, and there was nothing on which to focus except the drumbeat of his blood, hammering against his ears. Her hands were on him now, stroking, urging, pulling him toward a sweet wall of pain. There was something he needed— needed to do. Protection. He needed protection—for her. With his last bit of sense, he sheathed himself, then parted her legs and plunged inside.

After that, there was nothing but the ride and the destination.

Sometime before morning, Judd woke to find himself alone. After what they'd shared, the pain of abandonment was almost physical. He got out of bed and walked into the hall. The wet clothes they'd shed last night were nowhere in sight. The faint but steady hum of the washing machine told him what she'd been doing. Cleaning up so they wouldn't be caught. He wasn't sure whether he felt indignant that she wanted to hide what they'd done, or grateful that he wouldn't have to face the inevitable confrontation with Wade.

He looked in her room. It was empty. A faint light up the hallway led him into the living room. As he neared, he realized it was the lamp in the window. Left on, he supposed, for Wade, who had yet to come home. He shoved a hand through his hair in frustration. Where the hell could she be?

And then it hit him. Rachel. She must be in Rachel's room.

He backtracked his steps and peeked in the half-open door. Sure enough, she was there, dressed in a T-shirt with her long legs bare, rocking her sleeping baby by the beams of moonlight coming through windows. At his entrance, Charlie looked up.

"Is she all right?" he whispered.

She nodded, mouthing the words *bad dream.*

He smiled. He'd had a few of those in his time, himself. He pointed to the clock, mouthing the word *coffee* back at her.

She smiled to herself as he left. He was stark naked. She wondered if he realized it yet.

A few minutes later, she laid Rachel back in her crib, then tucked the favorite blanket under her chin. Rachel snuggled into it, rooting like a baby pig until she was satisfied with the feel, and promptly went back to sleep.

Charlie sighed with relief and tiptoed from the room. This didn't happen often, but when it did, nothing helped but a cuddle. She could hear Judd in the kitchen. Like a typical man, he was making more noise by trying to be quiet than he would have done if he'd behaved in a normal manner. She hugged the familiar sounds to herself, storing them in her mem-

ory for the time when he would be gone. As she
started up the hall, she remembered the gift that she'd
bought for him at the pharmacy and did a backtrack
to her room.

Judd was pouring his first cup of coffee when Charlie entered. He set it down and immediately held out
his arms. She went willingly, hiding the small box in
her hand.

"I didn't hear you get up," he said, then added,
"I missed you."

She closed her eyes, savoring the tenderness in his
voice.

"I hated to get up, too," she said. "I've never had
the pleasure of sleeping next to such a warm body."

He frowned. "Didn't you and—"

She didn't let him finish. "No. Pete wasn't into
sleeping with his women. Just screwing them."

Judd frowned. Her bitterness—when it came—always surprised him. She did a good job of hiding her
pain.

"Sorry," he said softly. "I didn't mean to bring
up bad memories."

She shook her head and smiled. "After last night,
I don't have room for any bad memories. From a
woman's point of view, you are perfect, Judd Hanna,
in every way that counts."

He took a deep breath. "Thank you, sweetheart."

"Oh, no. Believe me, the pleasure was all mine."

He grinned.

She poked at his bare belly in a teasing manner,
then tucked her finger in the waistband of his jeans
and gave them a tug.

"I have something for you," she said.

His smile widened. "Again?"

"Not that," she muttered. "Open your hand."

"What?"

"Just open your hand," she said, and then grabbed his wrist.

He obliged as she ordered, frowning slightly as she set a small box in the palm of his hand.

"What's this?" he asked.

"Open it and you'll see."

Oddly excited about the unexpected gift, he tore off the paper and tossed it aside, then opened the box. At once, his eyes widened and the grin on his face slipped and fell.

"Do you like it?" she asked, and without waiting for him to answer, took the watch out of the box and slipped it on his wrist. "If the band doesn't fit, you can take it to the pharmacy and Judith will fix it for you."

"It's Mickey Mouse," he said, swallowing past the lump in his throat, then tracing the path of the second hand with his finger as it swept around the face.

He was being so quiet, Charlie suddenly feared that he was embarrassed by the gift and didn't know how to tell her it was stupid.

"I know it's sort of silly, but I thought you could use a little fun in your life."

"When I was a kid, there was this fund-raiser contest at school. The student who sold the most candy bars would get a Mickey Mouse watch. I wanted that watch. More than I'd ever wanted anything in my life."

Charlie waited, knowing that the reason for his behavior would soon be clear.

"So, I peddled those candy bars up one street and

down another, working after school and on weekends until I'd sold twenty-seven boxes.''

He shifted the watch so that it would catch the light, staring in fascination at the little black mouse with the bright red pants.

''I knew I had it won. My closest competitor had only sold twelve. The day the contest came to an end, we were to turn in our money to the teacher. I was so excited I could hardly sleep. I could see myself walking to the front of the class and claiming my prize.''

Charlie was starting to tense. She could see the end of this story coming and the pain on his face nearly broke her heart.

''The next morning, as I was getting dressed for school, I went to the dresser to get the money, but it wasn't there. I'd been so careful, putting it in the same place every day when I came home. And even though I tore that room apart, telling myself that I'd just put it somewhere else by mistake, I already knew it was gone…and I knew who had taken it.'' He took a deep breath. ''It was one of the few times I ever yelled at him. I cursed and I cried and I screamed until my head was pounding. But it was no use. He couldn't have given it back to me if he'd wanted. He'd already spent it…on booze.''

''Oh, Judd. What happened?''

''I got in trouble at school. Everyone thought I'd either eaten all the candy myself, or sold it and kept the money. I was nine years old and I spent the rest of the semester cleaning toilets after school to pay back what he'd stolen.''

Then he looked at her, standing in the kitchen with no makeup and an old T-shirt on. Here was where the bloom was supposed to fall off the rose. Unfortunately for him, he thought she'd never looked better. At that point, he knew he was in trouble.

"There are no words to express what I'm feeling right now," he said gruffly. "But I feel it only fair to tell you that you could tick me off for the next twenty years, and it still wouldn't be enough to use up my joy."

She smiled. "See what you get when you give selflessly?"

"Yeah," he said. "The real dynamic duo...you and Mickey Mouse." He pulled her into his arms, crushing her close against his chest. "Damn woman, this is getting scary."

She sighed. "I know, Judd. I know."

It wasn't until a couple of days later that the UFO scare died down. By then, Judd and Charlie were feeling the desperation of the relationship. She woke up each morning, scared to death that this was going to be the day he would tell them goodbye, while he fell deeper and deeper in love. Somewhere in the midst of it all, something was going to have to give. And it did, right in the middle of Main Street at five minutes after twelve.

Judd sauntered out of the police department and headed for the café. He'd just gotten off the phone from talking to his captain, Roger Shaw, back in Tulsa. After Shaw had finished cursing at him, they'd settled down and had a fairly decent conversation. Bottom line, Judd had just let himself off the hook by turning in a verbal resignation, with a promise of a written one to follow. Now all he had to do was see if Wade had been serious about the job offer he'd made. And while he had yet to run it by Charlie, he was pretty sure she wouldn't mind if he stayed. Leaving Call City had become a thing of the past.

His step was light as he jogged across the street. Just as he got to the other side, he heard someone calling his name. He turned and then grinned. It was Davie, obviously on his way to the pharmacy, where Judith would be waiting to feed him his lunch.

"Hey, fella, how you been doing?" Judd asked.

"Got cans. Lotsa cans," Davie said, pointing into the wagon with pride.

"That you do," Judd said. "What are you going to buy with all that money?"

Davie frowned. "Something."

Judd sensed another secret looming, similar to the junkyard car that he'd favored.

"I keep secrets pretty good," Judd said. "Want to tell me?"

Davie shook his head. "No, I don't think so."

"That's all right," Judd said. "You're getting to be a big boy now, aren't you?"

Davie's face lit. "Yes. I'm a very big boy. Aunt Judy even let me use the lighter to burn the naked man's clothes."

Judd heard the words, but for a second, couldn't bring himself to respond. He took a deep breath, then squatted down, pretending to sift through the mound of crushed cans, giving himself time to think. But the longer he thought, the more certain he was that the mystery of Shuler's abduction had just been solved.

"So you burned them, did you?"

Davie nodded, but he was starting to frown. He'd

just remembered he wasn't supposed to talk about this.

"I have to go now," he said.

"Is that where you found Raymond's watch? The one you had to give back? Was it with the clothes your aunt Judy let you burn?"

"I'm not supposed to talk about this," Davie said, and started to cry.

Judd felt sick, both for what he'd just learned, and for the fact that two people he'd come to admire were at the bottom of a pretty serious crime.

"I know, son. I know."

He hesitated. Making a big deal out of this in the middle of the street would serve no purpose.

"You run along now. Your aunt probably has your lunch ready and waiting."

Davie looked relieved. "Yes. I will eat now." And he darted across the street without looking.

"Hey!" Judd yelled.

Davie stopped. When he turned, the innocence on his face made Judd sick.

"What?" he yelled.

"You forgot to look both ways before crossing the street," Judd warned.

"Oh! Yeah! I forgot. I will be careful again."

"Okay, buddy. Now, go eat your lunch."

As soon as Davie made the other side of the street to safety, Judd pivoted sharply and headed for the café to get Wade. No need being the only one who'd just had his lunch ruined.

Wade looked up from his BLT, grinning as he chewed. "I waited," he said, talking around a bite.

"I see you did," Judd said, and slid into the seat

opposite to the one where Wade was sitting. Then he leaned forward, lowering his voice so that he wouldn't be overheard. "We've got trouble," he said softly.

Wade rolled his eyes and then swallowed his bite, quickly washing it down with a big drink of iced tea.

"I almost hate to ask," he said.

"If you want Shuler's kidnappers, they're across the street at the pharmacy."

Wade sat up straight, his eyes wide with shock.

"The hell you say!" he yelled, then realized what he done. "Sorry," he said, tipping his hat to a couple of women in the next booth to apologize for his language. "The hell you say," he repeated in a much softer voice.

Judd waved a waitress away. "I'm not ordering," he said. "And he'll be needing his check."

Wade's mind was spinning. "We're not talking hostage situation here, are we? Do I need to notify the state police? Hell's bells, Judd. Tell me what's going on?"

"Let's get out of here," Judd said. "This is going to be public knowledge soon enough, but better later than now."

"My God," Wade muttered, and tossed some money down on the table as he followed Judd out the door.

As soon as they were alone on the street, he pulled Judd to one side.

"Talk to me."

Judd sighed. "I was talking to Davie just a couple of minutes ago. He was talking about secrets and buying things with his can money and accidentally blurted out that his aunt Judy let him burn the naked man's clothes."

Wade was speechless. He was hearing what Judd was saying, but his mind was not processing the facts.

Judd continued. "I asked Davie if that's where he found Raymond's watch. You know…in the clothes he was going to burn."

"What did he say?" Wade muttered.

"He got scared, realized he'd spoken out of turn and bolted for the pharmacy. I let him go. Figured the least I could do was let them have one last meal in peace before it hit the fan."

Wade wiped his hands across his face, then took off his hat and ran his fingers through his hair in disbelief.

"I have to be honest here, Judd. I don't quite know how to handle this. Yes, we could haul Davie in for further questioning, but in the eyes of the law, he's incompetent, so nothing he says will be of much use."

"But Judith might not know that," Judd said. "If you bring Davie in, I can guarantee she'll come to his rescue. If there's anything to what he just said, she'll tell the truth herself before she lets him suffer."

Wade nodded. "You're right about that."

"So, let's get this over with," Judd said.

Their hearts were heavy as they started across the street.

Chapter 13

Judith Dandridge knew before they opened their mouths that something was wrong. She'd never seen Wade so pale, and the new man, Judd Hanna, kept staring at Davie as if he were eating his last meal.

Suddenly, her heart skipped a beat. She didn't know how, but somehow, they knew. A strange calm came over her. Instead of panic, she felt an odd sense of relief.

"Gentlemen, how can I be of service?"

Wade was the one who spoke. "Judith, I'm going to have to ask you to bring Davie down to the police department."

The mention of Davie was a shock. Her voice started to shake.

"Why? What has he done?"

"We have reason to believe that he was involved in the kidnapping of Raymond Shuler."

"No," she moaned. "That's not so."

Davie heard the change in her voice and looked up, his sandwich forgotten.

"Aunt Judy...are you getting sick?"

She turned, the expression on her face pale and strained.

"No, dear. Finish your lunch."

"Yes, ma'am," he said, and took another bite.

"Please," she said. "You must be mistaken."

Judd shook his head. "No, ma'am, I'm not. A few minutes ago he told me that you let him start the fire that burned the naked man's clothes. So, unless you can produce proof that there's been another 'naked' man situation in this town in the past few days, I'm afraid the both of you are going to have to come with us."

Before she could answer, something crashed on the next aisle over. They turned in time to see a customer scurrying up the aisle toward the front door.

Judith swallowed a groan. That was Sophie Bruner, the biggest gossip in town. Within the hour, everyone would know. She glanced at Davie, in a panic as to what would happen to him when they took her away. But she didn't show her fear when she turned to them.

"If you'll give me a moment to gather up Davie's food, we'll be happy to come along."

Judd made no attempt to hide his surprise. She showed no remorse or fear. Then he thought of the altercations he'd witnessed between Judith and Shuler. While he didn't agree with what she'd done, he could almost understand it. The only thing that still puzzled him was the brand. What the hell did an *R* have to do with... He stopped in mid-thought. Revenge? Was it the symbol she'd left for revenge?

He watched her gentleness with Davie as she began

packing up his food, making it seem as if they were
going on a picnic so as not to frighten him. Poor
Davie—the world that he'd known was about to take
a terrible turn.

"Gentlemen," Judith said. "We're ready."

Wade opened the door for her. Judd followed them
up from the rear. Judith held Davie's hand as they
walked down the street, her expression revealing
nothing of her emotions, just as she'd been doing for
the last twenty years.

A few minutes later, she was seated at Wade's
desk. Judd watched from the doorway, waiting for
some sign of remorse. But Judith Dandridge's main
concern of the moment seemed to be that Davie not
spill his juice on Wade's floor.

"Judith, I'm going to be taping this," Wade said,
setting a tape recorder on his desk.

She shrugged. "Do what you have to do." Then
she grabbed for a chip that tumbled out of Davie's
hand. "Careful, sweetheart," she said softly. "We
don't want to get Wade's floor all dirty, do we?"

"Okay, Aunt Judy. I'll be careful."

"That's a good boy," she said softly, then looked
back at Wade, waiting for him to begin.

Wade glanced at Judd, his heart in his eyes. Judd
could only imagine how difficult it was for him to
arrest someone he'd known and respected for all these
years. Then Wade's eyes narrowed as he turned on
the recorder.

"This is Chief Wade Franklin, recording the interrogation of Judith Dandridge and her foster brother,
Davie Dandridge."

Judd watched a strange expression cross Judith's
face, but it came and went so quickly he thought he'd

imagined it. He glanced over his shoulder to the outer room, checking to make sure they wouldn't be disturbed, then nodded to Wade.

Wade took a deep breath.

"Judith Dandridge, you have the right to remain silent. If you choose to—"

She held up her hand. "I understand my rights," she said. "And I waive my right to have an attorney present."

He frowned and then shook his head. "As an officer, as well as your friend, I'm advising you to reconsider that last statement you made."

"I don't need a lawyer," she said. "All they do is make deals with other lawyers. No one pays any attention to the law as it is written anymore. If they had, none of this would be happening."

Judd felt sick to his stomach. There was a part of him that completely agreed with her. He couldn't think how many times he and his partner had arrested a perp, only to have him back out on the street before the day was over. He shoved the thought aside and refocused on the interview in progress.

"Judith, where were you on the night of August 5 of this year?" Wade asked.

"There's no need to pussyfoot through all of these questions," she said quietly. "I am the one responsible for teaching Raymond Shuler a lesson." Then she leaned over and wiped a bit of mustard from the edge of Davie's mouth.

Wade blinked. The admission wasn't exactly what he'd expected.

"You did more than teach him a lesson, Judith. You abducted him, held him against his will and inflicted bodily harm. Basically, that's called kidnapping, and it's a federal offense. Once we have your confession on tape, I'll have to notify the FBI. The case will be tried in federal court.''

"I tend to disagree with your description," she said. "I didn't kidnap him. Nothing was asked for, or traded for his release. When I thought he'd learned his lesson, I let him go. However, there's no need for a trial. I did it. I'll take whatever punishment the judge hands out.''

Wade cursed and got out of his chair, then turned off the recorder in frustration.

"Damn it to hell, Judith, have you completely lost your mind?''

She lifted her chin in a gesture of defiance. "Once, years ago," she said. "But I got over it.''

Davie began plucking at Judith's arm and trying to get her attention. All the yelling and tension was making him nervous.

"Aunt Judy…Aunt Judy…I need to go to the bathroom.''

"I'll take him," Judd said. "Come on, buddy. I'll show you where it is.''

"Thank you," she said, and then made Davie look at her. "Don't forget to wash your hands when you're through, and you come right back here to me.''

"Yes, ma'am," Davie said, and let Judd lead him away.

Judd stood in the hall outside the bathroom door, waiting for Davie to come out. And even from where he was standing, he could hear Wade, still yelling, and Judith, still answering in a calm, monotone voice. A few moments later, Davie emerged. He took Judd by the hand.

"Is my Aunt Judy mad at me?" he asked.

Judd shook his head. "No, Davie. If I had to guess, I'd say she's mad at herself."

"Okay," Davie said. "I'm ready now."

Halfway back to Wade's office, Raymond Shuler burst into the front door of the police department. His face was flushed in anger and he was already yelling before his wife, Betty, could shut the door behind them.

"Is it true?" he yelled. "Is Judith Dandridge the one responsible for my abduction?"

Judd bolted, trying to grab him before he barged into Wade's office, but he was too late to stop him.

"Get out, Shuler!" Wade said. "You have no business here."

"On the contrary," Judith said. "Let him stay. I don't mind."

Raymond stared. "You're crazy! Certifiably crazy!" he yelled, then waved his cane toward Davie, who'd come scurrying into the shelter of his aunt Judy's arms. "It's no wonder he turned out like he did."

Judith flinched but stood her ground.

Betty Shuler began to cry. "Judith, I just don't understand. I thought we were friends. Why on earth would you do something so horrible to my Raymond?"

Judith didn't bother to respond. Her attention was focused on Davie, who had started to sob.

"Look, Shuler," Judd said. "You've got a choice. Sit down and be quiet, or you're going to be arrested for disturbing the peace."

Betty dropped into a nearby chair, taking Raymond with her. He followed Judd's orders, but reluctantly.

Wade rolled his eyes. "This is the most unorthodox investigation I've ever seen."

"It was an unusual case," Judd said. "So far, it's sort of been resolving itself. Why don't we let it continue and see what happens?"

Wade picked up the recorder and waved it in everyone's face. "This will be on. Remember to mind your damned manners." He flipped the switch, then sat on the edge of his desk. "Judith, I'm going to ask this one more time, and by God, I want an answer. What prompted you to abduct Raymond Shuler?"

Judith turned, and the look she gave the banker made Judd's heart skip a beat.

"He was abusing his own son."

Raymond threw up his hands in disgust. "See, I told you, Wade. She's crazy. Everyone knows Betty and I have no children."

"I wasn't talking about you and Betty," she said. "I was talking about the baby I conceived after you raped me."

Raymond grunted audibly. Betty gasped. Wade and Judd looked at each other, then at Davie. And what was even more interesting to Judd was the fact that Raymond Shuler hadn't bothered to deny a rape had happened. In fact, the guilt on his face was obvious. Not only had he not denied it, but he couldn't bring himself to even look at the boy sitting beside Judith. Suddenly it was beginning to make sense. The *R* on Raymond's hip stood for *rapist*.

Wade touched Judith on the shoulder, waiting until she looked at him.

"Start at the beginning...please."

Judith sighed. "It was so long ago."

Her eyes lost focus, and Judd could tell she was no

longer here with them, but in a time when she'd still known how to smile.

"Everyone in school knew that Billy Ray Shuler always had to have his way." Then she looked up. "That's what we called him then…Billy Ray. He didn't become Raymond until he went to work at the bank. Anyway, he'd asked me out several times, but I wasn't interested."

Raymond finally regained his equilibrium enough to speak.

"I don't remember any rape," he muttered.

"I don't doubt that," Judith said. "I wish I could have said the same. It was homecoming night, two months before our senior graduation. You were blind drunk and mad because I'd gone out with Ted Miles instead of you."

She paused and looked up, explaining to Wade. "Ted was from Cheyenne. He came up from time to time to take me out. We were going to go to the university together."

Again, her gaze turned inward. Judd watched as her hands began to shake.

"Ted had been to the dentist that day. He wasn't feeling well and had gone home early from the game. I'd driven Daddy's old truck into town, so after the game was over, I started home." She took a deep breath, struggling with the panic that came from re-membering. "I had a flat," she muttered. "Some-times I wonder if I hadn't had that flat, what my life would have been like."

Then she shuddered. "Anyway…I had the flat, but no spare. We lived in the country then, out on the old Hamish place. I wasn't more than a mile from home, so I started to walk. It was a nice night. A three-quarter moon—nice breeze. I was actually enjoying the walk. And then the car came.''

Her hands suddenly fisted in her lap. ''It was Billy Ray, drunk out of his mind, and driving in the middle of the road. I got into the ditch, afraid that he was going to run over me.'' Her lips twisted bitterly. ''Looking back, that would have been preferable.''

Then she took a deep breath. ''He stopped. Offered me a ride. I told him no, that I didn't want to ride with him because he was drunk. The refusal angered him horribly. He got out of his car and started toward me, yelling about how I thought I was too good for the boys in Call City. I kept expecting him to pass out, but he didn't. I started to run. He caught me.''

Then she looked up, and the complete lack of expression in her voice was more horrible than any hysteria could have been.

''He broke my jaw and two ribs. He raped me in a foot of water and left me for dead. My daddy came looking for me around 3:00 a.m. He found the car first. They said I came stumbling out of the woods, bloody and in shock. That, I don't remember.'' She leaned forward, her gaze piercing Shuler with fierce intensity. ''My last memory was of his face and the pain between my legs as he tore into my body.''

Betty Shuler slid to the floor in a faint. Raymond was so stunned by what had been said that he sat and watched her fall. Oddly enough, it was Judith who offered advice.

''I have some smelling salts in my pharmacy. Should I get them for you?''

Wade sighed. ''No, ma'am. I think there're some in the first aid kit.'' He looked at Judd. ''Hold down the fort. I'll be right back.''

Judd nodded.

Raymond kept shaking his head, as if he couldn't accept what she'd said.

"Why didn't you say something?" he asked. "Why didn't you tell?"

"Oh, I did," she said. "I told Daddy. I expected justice, you see."

Raymond looked up at her then. "I don't get what you mean."

"Daddy didn't go to the police. He went to your father. Two weeks later, the mortgages on our home and Daddy's business were paid off and we had a new car."

A dark flush slid up Raymond's neck. "Are you saying my father paid your father off to keep his mouth shut?"

She sneered. "You're a banker, Raymond. Do the math."

Judd felt sick. He could identify with every injustice Judith Dandridge had suffered. As a child, he'd expected protection and justice from a parent, only to be the one to suffer at his hands, and had known that there was no one out there who would believe. He put his hand on Davie's shoulder.

"Judith, I'm assuming this is why you were home-schooled until graduation."

She nodded. "It was all I could do to make it through the ceremony. Every time I got around people, I became physically sick."

"Didn't your parents get you any counseling?"

She smiled bitterly. "Back then, counseling was for crazy people, and there was nothing wrong with me. I'd only been raped, remember?"

"There is no such thing as only rape," Wade said

as he came back into the room. "Judd, help me get Betty onto this sofa."

Together, they lifted Shuler's wife off the floor, then Wade broke the cylinder of smelling salts beneath her nose. Almost instantly, she roused. Once cognizance returned, she started to cry.

"Betty, I'm sorry," Raymond said. "You have to understand, I was just a kid. I didn't know what—"

"Shut up, Raymond," she said, sobbing. "You're always blaming someone else for your troubles, but this time, there's no one left but you to blame." Then she stood abruptly. "Wade...Mr. Hanna...if you will excuse me, I need to go now."

Wade shrugged. There was no reason she had to be there.

"You need a ride home?" he asked.

She clutched her purse to her chest, unable to look her husband in the face.

"No, it's Raymond who's going to be afoot when this is over."

Raymond looked startled, and it occurred to him then that he might be facing more than a revelation here. He might be facing divorce.

"Betty, you need to give me a chance to—"

"I don't need to do anything," she said, then turned to Judith. "I know it's not much, but I'm sorry," she said, and then walked out of the room.

Raymond struggled to his feet, torn between the need to follow his wife, and the fear of what else might be said if he left. He glanced at Wade.

"I don't intend to press charges," he said abruptly.

Wade sighed. Somehow he wasn't surprised. He looked at Judith. Her composure was frightening. She was far too cool for his peace of mind.

"That still doesn't eradicate the fact that she committed a crime," he said.

"I won't testify against her," Raymond muttered.

Judith sat quietly listening to the decisions men were making of her life. Then Raymond looked past her, for the first time since the revelation, to stare at the face of his child.

To his surprise, he actually recognized bits of himself. The dark hair. The nose, a little too short for the size of his face. The slight cleft in his chin. He blinked, surprised that he found himself crying.

"Boy."

Davie wouldn't look and Raymond couldn't blame him. He thought back to the treatment the boy had suffered at his hands.

"Boy, look at me…please," Raymond said.

Finally, he did.

"I promise I will never be mean to you again."

The slow smile that came on Davie's face shamed Raymond more than he could say. Then he looked at Judith.

"Sorry will never be enough," he said. "If there is ever anything I can do for you…or for him…"

"Davie. His name is Davie," Judith said shortly.

Raymond flinched as he spoke the name, for the first time in his life, saying the name of his son aloud.

"Davie. If there is ever anything I can do for Davie, all you have to do is ask."

"Just leave us alone," she said.

His shoulders slumped. He walked out of the department, a lesser man than when he'd come in.

Judd looked at Wade, waiting for him to make the call.

Wade leaned forward.

"Judith, you know you need some help."

She shrugged. "Once I needed help and no one came."

Judd's belly turned. With that one sentence, he was yanked back to that place beneath the stairs where he'd prayed to God for help that never came. He took a deep breath, fighting the nausea that came up in his throat.

"That may be so," Wade said. "But I'm talking about now. Who's to say you don't fly off the deep end and do something worse the next time?"

"There won't be a next time," she said. "I accomplished what I set out to do."

Judd's breath was coming faster now. He could feel himself coming undone. Everything Wade was saying to Judith, his captain had said about him. He'd ignored it then, refusing to believe it of himself. But now, faced with the evidence of what suppressed anger could do, he knew his troubles were not over. Not until he faced his own devil as Judith Dandridge had done.

"I don't intend to argue about this," Wade said. "I'm going to recommend that you start some counseling. Only after I'm convinced that you've channeled your need for revenge into something positive, I'll consider the case closed. Do we have a deal?"

Judith stood. "Since I have no say in this matter, I suppose we do." Then she began gathering up the remains of Davie's lunch.

"Is the picnic over, Aunt Judy?" Davie asked.

She stopped, staring at him for a long, silent moment, then she ruffled his hair.

"Yes, dear, I believe the picnic is finally over."

Judd couldn't be there any longer. He needed to move, before he came undone.

"I'll be at the house," he said shortly, and stalked out of the office before Wade could object.

All the way home, he kept seeing himself as a child, storing away the hate because it was all his father could give him. He thought of Charlotte, and of Rachel's sweet baby face. Always laughing, in constant mischief. Neither one of them deserved to live with a ticking time bomb, which is what he knew he was.

By the time he turned in the driveway, he knew what he had to do.

Charlie was still in shock when Judd pulled up in front of the house and parked. Wade's call wasn't unusual, but his news had floored her. Not only had he called to tell her that he wouldn't be home until he was certain the news didn't start a riot in the streets, he'd felt obligated to warn her that Judd had bolted out of the office without an explanation and was on his way there.

She heard Judd get out, then heard the car door slam shut. She glanced at the clock. It was just after one. Rachel would nap for at least another hour, maybe longer. That was good. She and Judd could talk. He was obviously upset about something, or he wouldn't have left so abruptly. She wouldn't let herself think of the inevitable—that the mystery was solved and he would be leaving. She wouldn't think about that at all.

She heard the kitchen door open. She turned. Judd was standing in the door and she could tell by the look on his face that he had come to say goodbye.

"This isn't fair," she whispered.

"Life rarely is," he countered, and took her in his arms.

She clung to him, stifling an urge to throw herself at his feet and beg him to stay, but her pride was all she had left. It would be what held her together when he was gone.

"Wade told me what happened."

Judd shook his head. "It was unbelievable."

She pushed out of his embrace and then turned, reaching for a dish towel to have something to hold besides him.

"I suppose you came to pack your things." And then her chin quivered. "In a way, I've been expecting this," she said. "Only not quite so sudden."

Judd sighed. Of course she was going to misunderstand. If only he could make her see.

"It's not what you think," he said softly.

She turned, clutching the dish towel against her belly, her eyes nearly blind with tears.

"Then make me understand," she said. "Because I'm thinking that I just might die from this pain."

He groaned. "God, Charlotte, I need to do this or I'll wind up like her."

She frowned. "Like who?"

"Judith. Judith Dandridge. If I don't get rid of the hate that's inside me, I'm afraid that one day I'll explode as she did—only you and Rachel would be the ones who would suffer."

She blanched. Suddenly, things were starting to make sense. This wasn't about him leaving her. It was about finishing the journey he'd started before they met.

She swiped at her tears with the flats of her hands.

"I have a request to make of you."

"Ask," he said.

"Go bury your demons and lay all your ghosts, Judd Hanna, but when you're through, will you come back to me?"

"In a heartbeat," he said, then pulled her back into his arms. "Now I have a request to make of you."

"Ask."

"Lie with me, love."

"Always," she answered, and wrapped her arms around his neck.

Two hours later, he was gone. Charlie was still crying when Rachel woke up from her nap. She toddled into the room, dragging her blanket behind her as she went and crawled into her mother's lap.

"'Mallows?" she asked, and then laid her head on Charlie's breast, uncomfortable with the tears on her mother's face.

Charlie hugged her close, struggling to remember where her priorities lay.

"Okay, sweetheart," she said. "We'll go get you some 'mallows."

Rachel grinned, pleased with the answer. "Judd have some, too?"

Charlie stifled a sob. "Not today, honey. Judd went bye-bye. He'll have to eat his 'mallows somewhere else."

Chapter 14

More than a week had passed since Judd's exit from Call City. He'd stopped in Tulsa on his way through and tied up the last of loose ends. The news that they'd arrested the perp who'd killed his partner was a huge relief. Everyone at the police department had seemed genuinely glad to see him, but he'd already felt the mental distance between them. He'd abandoned them. They'd gone on with their lives. It was the way things were.

After that, it had taken him a couple more days to pack up his apartment and put the stuff in storage. Now there was nothing standing between him and Charlie but the laying of ghosts.

The next day, he'd packed up his car and headed east, telling himself that the anxiety he felt was all in his mind. Yet the minute he crossed the border into Kentucky, his belly started to knot. He couldn't see the rich green of the mountains or the deep, endless valleys for the memories that came flooding back. It had been fifteen years since he'd gotten on that bus in Paducah, determined that life would not turn him into a replica of his father. And in a manner of speaking it had not. But something had happened to him along the way that he hadn't expected. His father had given him up, but Judd had never given up the hate that bound them. Normally, one would expect the years to fade a child's memories, but not so Judd's. Some of the foster homes he'd been put in were good, some not so good. But nothing had ever come close to the hell of his first ten years.

He stopped at a gas station along the highway to refuel. And as he waited for the car to fill up, his gaze fell on a telephone booth beside the store. Immediately, his thoughts went to Charlie. Was she okay? How long would it be before Rachel would forget him? He sighed. The deputy was probably back from his honeymoon by now. Oh, God, please don't let Charlie have second thoughts now that I'm gone.

The pump kicked off and he replaced the nozzle before going to pay. The day was warm, the wind, gusting. When he got inside, he went to the cooler to get something to drink, then strolled past the small grocery aisle to pick up a bag of chips. As he did, a display of marshmallows caught his attention and he immediately thought of Rachel. She was quite a charmer. If they had a houseful like her it would be great.

Then he stopped, overwhelmed by the idea of family, and of knowing that he would always be loved. The concept was staggering to a man who'd never known it before.

''Will that be all, mister?''

Judd looked up. The woman behind the cash register was waiting. He set his purchases down on the counter, then pulled out his wallet. A short while later, he was back on the road. If he'd figured correctly, he would be in Boyington by midafternoon. Soon enough to find a motel—and call Charlotte. He just needed to hear her voice. After that, he would take it one day at a time.

Wade sat at the kitchen table, helping Rachel eat a bowl of spaghetti, while eyeing Charlie's every move. He knew she was worried. It had been a week since Judd's departure and they had yet to hear from him. But every time he brought up the subject, she gave him the same explanation, saying Judd would be back.

"How do you know?" Wade had asked, and her answer was always the same. "Because he said."

She was running on nerves and he could tell it, but there was nothing he could say to make it better.

A short while later, they were just sitting down to their supper when the phone began to ring. Charlie jerked, dropping a fork she'd been about to put in the salad, then turned, staring at the phone as if she could will it to be Judd.

"I'll get it," Wade said, and reached for the phone. "Hello, this is Wade."

"Is Charlie there?"

Wade let out a sigh of relief. "Breathing down my neck. I suppose you want to talk to her instead of me."

"Sorry," Judd said. "But you just don't have what it takes."

"That's not what the new waitress at the Call City café thinks," Wade said.

Judd laughed in his ear. Wade grinned as he handed the phone to Charlie.

"For you, sis."

"Hello?"

"Charlotte, is your brother still listening?"

Weak with relief, she leaned against the wall and cupped the phone against her ear.

"No."

"Good," Judd said. "Because what I have to say to you isn't fit for other ears."

She grinned. "I'm listening."

Moments later, her eyes widened, and then her heart skipped a beat.

"Is that possible?" she muttered.

"Oh, yeah," Judd said. "And after that, I'm going to…"

Charlie moaned beneath her breath.

"Are you all right?" Wade asked.

She nodded, then laughed out loud. "I am now."

Judd smiled to himself, listening to the joy in her voice and knowing that he'd made the right decision to call.

"I miss you, Charlotte. I miss seeing you, and touching you. I miss your smile, and the way you chew on your lower lip when you're bothered."

"I miss you, too," she said, echoing his sentiments. Then she added, "Are you okay? I mean… have you found what you were looking for?"

He glanced at the phone book, and the name he'd circled in red.

"Not yet, but I'm close."

She sighed. "Take care and hurry home."

The words wrapped around him. Home. Hurry home.

"Keep the bed warm for me," he said softly.

"Always," she said.

Moments later, he was gone.

Wade was grinning. "So he called. So I was wrong. So sue me."

Charlie sat down at the table, then sighed. She wasn't going to relax until he was back in her arms.

Morning was a long time coming. Judd had walked the motel floor until long after 1:00 a.m., psyching himself up. More than once he found himself standing in front of the mirror, staring at his reflection.

He was a big man—well over six foot tall. His shoulders were broad, sometimes too broad for the clothes on the racks. He'd been shot once and broken his leg twice. Once while running down a perp, and the second time, falling off a dock at Lake Tenkiller while fishing for crappie. He'd had two partners in his law enforcement career, and both were dead. One of natural causes, the other died on the job. Both times, he stood at the gravesite, dry-eyed and stoic. He was the iron man. The man who never gave up.

Finally, he turned away from the mirror, unable to look at himself anymore. If he was so damned tough, then why was he scared to death to go face the bogeyman down? He wasn't a kid any longer. On a daily basis he had arrested worse men than Joe Hanna and had never flinched. But Judd was overlooking one very important fact. His only knowledge of Joe had come when he was a child, too small to fight back. There were no mental boundaries for the man Joe was today.

He reached for his jacket and started to put it on, then decided against it and tossed it back on the bed.

"Just get it over with," he muttered, and headed for the door before he could talk himself out of the trip.

An hour later, he was cruising through the streets, checking addresses and looking for something—anything—that might prove familiar. But it had been a long time. Things change. People move. Houses get remodeled and some even burn down, which was the case with the house he'd just passed. He slowed, leaning forward and peering out the windshield as he checked the house numbers for 122. And a few minutes later, he saw it, then tapped the brakes and wheeled up to the curb.

The house was old, like the one they'd lived in when he was a kid, but it was different. He didn't recognize anything about where he was—not the neighborhood, not the landscape, not any of the nearby businesses he'd passed. Maybe he had the wrong man, or the right man and the wrong address, or maybe he was just delaying the inevitable. He sighed. Most likely the latter.

He got out, slamming the door shut behind him, then stood for a moment, his hands on his hips, his Stetson pulled down low across his forehead. Even though he had parked in the shade, the air was already hot. He was glad he'd left his jacket behind.

The house at 122 May Avenue was in need of paint. The screens on the windows were rusted, giving the gray, peeling house the appearance of having black eyes. Large trees shaded the small, postage-stamp yard, and tall, overgrown bushes in desperate need of trimming bordered the old concrete porch. There was a narrow opening in the bushes that led to the steps, and then the front door. He fixed his gaze and started toward it with purpose in his step.

By the time he got to the front door, he was sick to his stomach. He kept picturing a large, angry man looming over him in the dark. He made a fist and started to knock, when he was startled by a voice to his left.

"What's your business?"

He jerked, his hand automatically going for a gun that wasn't there. He squinted, peering into the shadows, and could just make out the silhouette of an old man in a chair.

"I'm looking for a man," Judd said.

The old man snorted. "One of them kind, are ye?"

Judd frowned, ignoring the allusion to homosexuality.

"His name is Joe Hanna. Do you know him?"

This question seemed to set the old man into hysterics. He slapped his leg and guffawed until he made himself cough. Then he hacked for another minute or so until Judd thought he was going to have to call an ambulance.

"You all right?" Judd asked.

The old man pounded his chest, wheezing and gasping as he shook his head.

"Hell, no, I ain't all right. I'm dying," he muttered.

"Still got your sense of humor," Judd said.

The old man grinned. "Well, I ain't dead yet."

Judd started all over again. "About Joe Hanna. The name in the phone book lists him at this address. Do you know how long he's been gone?"

The old man laughed again, slapping his leg and rocking back in his chair.

Judd rolled his eyes, waiting for the mirth to subside. Obviously, the old fellow knew something that Judd did not.

Finally, the old fellow calmed. Judd asked him again.

"Please, mister. It's important to me. Do you know where I can find Joe Hanna?"

The old man leaned forward, pointing at Judd with a long, bony finger.

"Who wants to know?" he asked.

Judd pulled out his ID, wishing at the moment that he still had his badge, but he'd already turned that in to the captain back in Tulsa.

The old man waved Judd's wallet away.

"I can't see nothin' anymore. Talk to me, boy. I ain't in the mood to read a book."

"I'm a cop. My name is Judd Hanna, and I'm looking for a man named—"

"Joe."

"Right," Judd said. "Joe Hanna."

The old man's expression was suddenly haggard. Judd wondered what it would be like to accept the imminence of death, to take each breath knowing it could be the last. He watched as the old man dragged himself to his feet, then began an odd little scoot and sidestep toward where Judd was standing.

But the closer he got, the more tense Judd became. He didn't know when he finally realized his search was over, but as he did, a bonus came with it. The fear he'd been saving for all of these years wasn't there. Joseph Hanna, the snarling demon who'd plagued his life and his dreams, didn't even have his own teeth anymore. Judd took a deep, cleansing breath, then looked down into the face of his father.

"I didn't figure on ever seeing you again," Joe said.

"I didn't plan to come."

The abruptness of his son's answer wasn't what Joe expected. Like Judd, he didn't know how to relate. This wasn't the little snot-nosed kid who'd caused him so much trouble. This man was tall, much taller than Joe had ever been, and there was an edge to his manner that Joe envied. A "like me or leave me alone" attitude he'd never been able to cultivate. In that moment, he would have sold his soul for the ability to stand straight once again. And then he amended the thought. Hell, he couldn't sell something he'd already lost.

"So…if this little surprise ain't no accident, then what are you doing here?" Joe asked.

Judd thrust his hands in his pockets.

"Laying ghosts."

Joe frowned. "I don't get it."

Judd shrugged. "Somehow, that doesn't surprise me, old man."

"Yeah, you call me old now, but once I was big and strong and—"

"And you beat the hell out of me for no reason. Every day of my life, just because you could. Yeah, you're right old man, once you were a real, big son of a bitch."

Joe looked flustered, then became defensive.

"I did the best I could," he said. "It wasn't easy raisin' no kid by myself."

"You didn't raise me. I took care of myself."

"You don't know nothin'," Joe muttered.

Judd sighed, suddenly exhausted, as if he'd been awake forever.

"Maybe you're right. But what I do know is that I guess what I came for was to tell you goodbye."

Joe blinked. "But you just got here."

"You're wrong. I never left—at least, not in my mind. It's past time I let it all go."

He settled his hat a little firmer upon his head and turned away.

"Where you goin'?"

Judd paused, then turned. "I'm going home, where I belong."

Joe followed him to the edge of the steps, watching the vigor with which Judd was walking, and in that moment, resented him more than he'd ever resented him before.

"You think you're something, don't you?" Joe yelled. "You think because you're bigger and meaner now, that you're top dog. Well, I got news for you. You'll never be like me, boy! Never!"

Halfway down the sidewalk, Judd stopped and turned, and there was a look on his face that had never been there before.

"Thanks—Dad. That's the best news you ever gave me."

Then he got in his Jeep and drove away. The farther he got, the lighter his heart became. He'd buried his demons—conquered his fears. It had taken him twenty-three years, but he'd vanquished the monster under the bed.

He'd been on the road for two days, driving almost nonstop. The urge to get back to Charlie was fierce, far stronger than the one that had taken him away.

He glanced at his watch, judging his exhaustion against the time it would take him to reach Call City. He groaned. At the least, it was another three hours of hard driving. Ahead, a line of thunderstorms were lighting up the sky—ripping apart the heavens with bright angry threads of pure energy. If he kept going, he'd be driving straight into the mess. There was a small town up ahead. He remembered it from before, when he'd first come this way. It had a motel. He could stay there for the night and get an early start tomorrow. But the thought of being only a few hours away from Charlotte's arms was enough to keep him driving.

Another hour passed, and true to his prediction, he had driven into the storm. The force of the wind was whipping his Jeep all over the road, and it was all he could do to keep it in the right lane. The frenzy of the windshield wipers scraping back and forth across the glass beat a rhythm he couldn't ignore.

Char-lie. Char-lie.

Everything whispered her name.

"Just get me home," Judd said, unaware that he'd said the words aloud until the sound of his own voice startled him.

And as he focused on what he'd just said, his heart skipped a beat. Dear God. While he'd been a little vague about who he'd been asking, he'd just said a prayer. Something he hadn't done since that night under the stairs.

Granted, as far as prayers went, it wasn't much, but for a man who'd all but given up on God, it was a giant step in the right direction. The emotional upheaval of the revelation left him stunned. Where had the urge come from?

Was it something as simple as going home to Charlie? Was that what he had needed to regain his faith? Or was it the fact that he'd turned loose of his hate and would no longer be haunted by visions of Joe Hanna's face? He cleared his throat, a little stunned that his eyes had filled with tears.

"Are you there, God? It's been a real long time since I acknowledged your presence."

His heart stayed silent. If there were answers, Judd couldn't hear them.

Suddenly, a bolt of lightning hit the ground a short distance ahead. Judd swerved, almost running off the road. As he guided the vehicle from the shoulder, then back to the highway, he breathed a quick sigh of relief, realizing he'd just gotten an answer.

"Thanks," he said softly. "I owe you one."

He continued to drive, never taking his gaze from the yellow line that was leading him back to Charlie.

The thunderstorm had passed through hours ago, washing everything clean. Outside the Franklin homestead, water stood in puddles, reflecting the moon glow overhead. Except for Wade's occasional snore and the tick of a clock, the house was silent.

And then in the middle of a breath, Charlie sat bolt upright, looking around the room in sudden panic. What? What was it she'd heard?

She threw back the covers and raced out of the room; her first instinct, as always, was Rachel. But her baby was asleep, motionless beneath the wrap she'd made of her blanket. She stood in the hallway a moment, listening closer, yet heard nothing but Wade's gentle snores. She turned, looking nervously up the hall. Something was going to happen, she just knew it, but what could it be?

Hugging herself quickly, she started to go back to bed, but the moment she turned her back on the hall, the feeling came over her again.

"God, I know that you're here...but I don't know what you're trying to say."

Knowing now that sleep would be impossible, she tiptoed up the hall, following the glow from the living room lamp, and curled up in one of the chairs. Her eyes were wide, transfixed by the darkness beyond the windows as she waited for the answer to be revealed.

Judd's eyes were heavy, his body weary from lack of sleep, but the urge to keep moving was strong— so strong. Two packages sat on the seat beside him, each wrapped in a different color of paper. In the pink one, all covered with ribbons and curls, was a small baby doll with its very own blanket and wide brown eyes, just like a certain baby he knew. The package of miniature marshmallows it was pillowed on was probably getting squashed, but Judd knew she wouldn't object.

The white package was small and unadorned, but to Judd, it held the greatest treasure of all—Charlotte's ring. He'd dreamed of putting it on her finger, of watching the expression on her face spreading from surprise to joy. It was to be the final connection needed that would bind him to these people for the rest of their lives.

A ring, two simple words, and a preacher. That's all it would take. And the only thing left between them was a slow but diminishing distance.

Suddenly, Judd straightened in the seat as he realized he was beginning to recognize landmarks. Even in the dark, he could see the outline of Old Man Tucker's barn. And down the road was the tree with three forks. His heart skipped a beat.

Another mile, then another, and without warning, the road was there. He took the turn, following the beam of his headlights as they cut through the night. In the midst of his anticipation, it hit him that, although he had reached his destination, they would all be asleep.

And then he topped the hill leading down toward the house, and his heart caught in his throat. There, shining through the old farmhouse window, was that lamp, burning bright against the night. Tears shattered his vision, bringing him and the Jeep to a halt. In the distance, he could see the faint outline of Wade's patrol cruiser and Charlie's car. Everyone was home—except him. He took a deep breath. With the lamp as a guide, he began to move.

Charlie was staring blindly through the windows when she first saw the headlights top the hill. And the moment she did, she was on her feet and running for the door. This was her answer. This was why she'd wakened so abruptly in the middle of the night.

She ran outside, standing at the edge of the steps and watching as the vehicle came to a stop. She bolted off the porch as the man inside emerged. Within seconds, she was in his arms, crying and laughing as she fielded his kisses.

"You're home! You're home! Thank God, you're finally home."

Judd's heart was full to overflowing. A thousand

words were running through his mind and all he could do was hold her. The softness of her body, the tenderness of her touch—even the laughter she had saved for him—were almost more than he could bear. He kept taking deep breaths between kisses, wanting to tell her, needing her to know that she was his true partner, that she had saved him, as surely as if she'd stood armed at his back, but nothing came out of his mouth but her name.

Charlie paused in the middle of a kiss, laughing as she cupped his face with her hands.

"Yes, Judd Hanna, it's me. Welcome home, my darling, welcome home."

*   *   *   *   *

If you enjoyed what you just read,
then we've got an offer you can't resist!

Take 2 bestselling love stories FREE!
Plus get a FREE surprise gift!

Clip this page and mail it to Silhouette Reader Service™

IN U.S.A.
3010 Walden Ave.
P.O. Box 1867
Buffalo, N.Y. 14240-1867

IN CANADA
P.O. Box 609
Fort Erie, Ontario
L2A 5X3

YES! Please send me 2 free Silhouette Intimate Moments® novels and my free surprise gift. Then send me 6 brand-new novels every month, which I will receive months before they're available in stores. In the U.S.A., bill me at the bargain price of $3.57 plus 25¢ delivery per book and applicable sales tax, if any*. In Canada, bill me at the bargain price of $3.96 plus 25¢ delivery per book and applicable taxes**. That's the complete price and a savings of over 10% off the cover prices—what a great deal! I understand that accepting the 2 free books and gift places me under no obligation ever to buy any books. I can always return a shipment and cancel at any time. Even if I never buy another book from Silhouette, the 2 free books and gift are mine to keep forever. So why not take us up on our invitation. You'll be glad you did!

245 SEN CNFF
345 SEN CNFG

Name	(PLEASE PRINT)	
Address	Apt.#	
City	State/Prov.	Zip/Postal Code

* Terms and prices subject to change without notice. Sales tax applicable in N.Y.
** Canadian residents will be charged applicable provincial taxes and GST.
   All orders subject to approval. Offer limited to one per household.
   ® are registered trademarks of Harlequin Enterprises Limited.

INMOM99   ©1998 Harlequin Enterprises Limited

Don't miss Silhouette's newest cross-line promotion,

Four royal sisters find their own Prince Charmings as they embark on separate journeys to find their missing brother, the Crown Prince!

Royally Wed

The search begins in October 1999 and continues through February 2000:

On sale October 1999: **A ROYAL BABY ON THE WAY** by award-winning author **Susan Mallery** (Special Edition)

On sale November 1999: **UNDERCOVER PRINCESS** by bestselling author **Suzanne Brockmann** (Intimate Moments)

On sale December 1999: **THE PRINCESS'S WHITE KNIGHT** by popular author **Carla Cassidy** (Romance)

On sale January 2000: **THE PREGNANT PRINCESS** by rising star **Anne Marie Winston** (Desire)

On sale February 2000: **MAN...MERCENARY...MONARCH** by top-notch talent **Joan Elliott Pickart** (Special Edition)

ROYALLY WED
Only in—
SILHOUETTE BOOKS

Available at your favorite retail outlet.

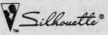

Visit us at www.romance.net

SSERW

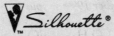

MONTANA MAVERICKS
Big Sky Brides

Legendary love comes to Whitehorn, Montana,
once more as beloved authors

Christine Rimmer, Jennifer Greene and Cheryl St.John

present three brand-new stories in this exciting anthology!

Meet the Brennan women:
SUZANNA, DIANA and ISABELLE

Strong-willed beauties who find unexpected
love in these irresistible marriage of
covnenience stories.

Don't miss
MONTANA MAVERICKS: BIG SKY BRIDES
On sale in February 2000,
only from Silhouette Books!

Available at your favorite retail outlet.

Silhouette®

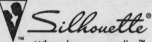